All Down The Line

Andrew Field

This edition published in 2020 by
Boomslang Books

26 Mill Wharf

Tweedmouth

Berwick upon Tweed

Northumberland

TD15 2BP

Copyright © Andrew Field
www.boomslangbooks.org

ISBN: 978-1-9999826-9-0

For Nick F ... TKO too early

'Everyone has a plan until they get punched in the mouth.'

Mike Tyson & Nick Forti

'Manchester is the only English City which can look London in the face, not merely as a regional capital but as a rival version of how man should live in a community.'

AJP Taylor

One.

2017: two-glasses Chablis confident. His tall body twelve percent alcohol by volume euphoric. Anything was possible. Until the grape short-circuited limbs, mind and memory. Cain Bell didn't take chances. Perrier diluted the wine. The question must be popped straight. Pissed was pathetic. Once Little Miss Red Dress gave him the thumbs up he would swing into action. Only he couldn't see her: that worried him.

He sipped water and wine. Thirty quid retail. He paid full price. Like every punter. House rules. No freebies. No discounts. No exceptions. Every transaction tracked by an electronic point of sale system time-linked to CCTV. The digital combo eliminated theft. Kept people honest. Every receipt and invoice double-checked and cross-referenced. Every menu and margin interrogated. April Sands' obsessive attention to detail was mirrored by his own.

He loved her OCD instincts. He loved every inch of her, inside and out. Watching her sent shivers down his long spine. Released rioting butterflies in his stomach. She stood there loud and proud, larger than life on a small music stage.

Next to her was the queen of free scran, the supersize food editor of the evening newspaper who never turned down second helpings of pudding, or anything else you could swallow. She was a heavyweight hedonist legend. What she didn't know about scoffing could be written on the left wing of a bumble bee.

April clutched a bronze capital M embedded in a square wooden dining plate. Thanked Manchester for naming the Red Manifesto its best restaurant. Made a promise. 'This time next year we want a Michelin star. You live in the best city in the world and deserve the very best.'

Everybody cheered. April milked the applause. Paused her speech until the clapping subsided. Cain knew he was looking at the most wonderful woman in the world.

He often told his mates his words could never do her justice. He was not a good enough writer. They laughed at his Mancunian humour, although he meant it. He had a question but needed the approval of Little Miss Red Dress: where was the little tyke?

He scanned the restaurant. Madam was playing hide and seek. He checked the crowded staircase. Standing room only. He was annoyed. Little Miss Red Dress should share the moment: silly girl, not her fault, nothing was.

'Daddy.' A half-heard whisper drew him back to the staircase. She was standing between two of his security guys. Pyramid-shaped chaps with thick necks. Scoffed steroids like smarties. She waved at him. He smiled. Raised a glass of Perrier. Toasted her good health. She grinned. 'It's OK, Daddy. I love April very much.'

He silently mouthed he loved her too. The security chaps

grinned back. Gave him the thumbs-up. Semi-took the piss as men-children do when their measurement of strength was the number of times you could lift your body weight on a bench press before you shat yourself.

Approved, Cain stood up. His chair scraped on the wooden floor. The unexpected noise temporarily stopped her words. She turned and glared to see who had dared interrupt her. Looked straight at him. Head slightly tilted to compensate for her blind left eye. A flash of anger was replaced by a reassuring wink. Like a true pro, she adapted her acceptance speech without missing a beat. 'There are lots of people involved in the Red Manifesto project who can take pride in this award but none more so than my business partner and best friend, Cain Bell. Join me on the stage.'

'No, it's your moment,' he said, as he took several steps towards her. 'Your achievement. Your idea. Your hard work.'

'Without you, it's nothing,' she replied. Her smile as bright as a lighthouse beam warning ships about dangerous rocks hidden under calm seas.

He stopped. Glanced over at the staircase. Little Miss Red Dress encouraged him. Excitement was written large across her pretty face. He looked back at April, eyes on the grand prize. 'Will you marry me?'

Immediately, the gob-smacked pan-American restaurant guests were transfixed. The stakes were upped from an ugly trophy to matrimony. She said nothing. Looked as surprised as they did.

'Wow,' said a lone voice in amazement.

'As a humanist I don't believe a woman should take a man's name, but this feels so, so right.'

'Double wow,' said another voice.

3

Cain navigated the chairs and tables between the bar and the stage. As he reached the last three steps, self-doubt bit him on the bum. They had never discussed marriage. Never even joked about tying the knot during early morning breakfast and broadsheet chats in their penthouse.

Ticklish butterfly wings flapped inside his guts. Vertebrae tingled up and down his backbone. What if April turned him down? How embarrassing would that be? Especially if the failed public proposal went viral. At least one customer would have filmed his humiliation. Millions would laugh at him.

He dropped lightly onto one knee. He held her hands in his. Hoped the contact would yield a clue to her answer to his repeated question. 'Will you please be my wife?'

To be honest, he felt totally out of his depth with April Sands. She was headline news. A celebrity chef and former global Madchester party girl once married to a Hollywood film producer. Had her own Wikipedia page. She reflected modern Manchester: a sassy, sexy European hub. Owned property in Manchattan, the intended home to half a dozen giant skyscrapers that would redefine the city's skyline.

Cain mirrored the dirty old town of the sixties and seventies. A post-modern ironic refuge bumming the price of a cup of Earl Grey. Cain didn't have his own Wikipedia page. Wasn't mentioned on hers, either. One of life's natural born wingmen. The journalist reporting on people more famous. The PR man standing in the shadows, pushing others into the spotlight. A former father watching other men play with their young children.

None of that mattered.

He had seriously misread the situation. Her silence spoke

volumes. He was fun, a laugh and good company. Not the type to marry. Normally he planned things better: both in his day job as a public relations officer at Global Manchester — and his side-hustle, marketing the restaurant to the city's well-heeled elite. Momentarily, he hoped Little Miss Red Dress had returned to save him from public humiliation.

'Yes,' she said. Did he hear her right? Yes, she would, or yes, she wouldn't? Play it again. 'Yes. I'll be honoured to be your wife, Mr Cain Bell.'

Applause bounced off exposed brick walls. 'I was so excited I forgot the ring,' said Cain. He would tell her the truth later. They had no secrets, or so he thought. He had only decided to propose earlier in the day. Not even had time to discuss it with anyone apart from Little Miss Red Dress.

'All I want is you,' she said. They kissed. Phones captured the moment; images and videos posted, liked and shared on social media the instant their lips touched. She leaned into him. Spoke only for his ears. 'I must tell you something before we makes promises to God we cannot keep.'

'Don't understand,' said Cain.

'Should have told you ages ago.'

'Why didn't you?'

'Never the right time.'

'And now is, when I've just proposed?'

'If you want us to marry, yes.'

'Whisper them to me now, quickly,' said Cain, thirty quid a bottle Chablis confidence flushed down the pan. Something was up. She had secrets in places where he thought they only had unconditional love.

'Not in public. At home. Will take more than a couple

of rushed sentences to explain. There is so much to tell you. You might not love me as much, once you know the truth. You deserve better than my lies.'

She pulled away. Broke the embrace. He let her. He felt awkward and confused. He squeezed her hand hard. Can he edit the action so it played out more to his liking?

Something he won't like? What was that meant to mean?

Nothing she said could diminish his love for her. He had to tell the world.

'I am proud to be here in front of you, my friends and colleagues, fellow Mancs. Same pride I felt when my daughter was born.'

'I've lived life hard and fast. I've always worked with a tab in one hand and a glass in the other. Great lifestyle when you're a stick insect without a care in the world … not so smart when you are a lard in your forties. Would have paid the ultimate price but for this wonderful lady standing by my side. She literally saved me when the old ticker stopped in protest at my hedonistic lifestyle. She glued my head back together piece by piece. She has given me purpose. Hopefully, I can repay her faith.'

That was a fine speech. Words were his forte. His weapon of choice. Protected him when he needed to defend himself. But misused words could knock the stuffing out of you. Just like the words delivered by April. Why would he hate her after she told him the truth about herself?

The applause had subsided. He held April's hand aloft to ramp up the volume. There had to be an explanation.

What could she do to make him hate her when he knew she was the most beautiful woman in the world?

Two.

Cain's natural instinct was to leave the party after the victory salute, except April appeared to have forgotten their brief conversation. Throwing a public tantrum would make him look like a puerile paranoid prat. Instead, he silently seethed while the busy network queen floated like a butterfly and stung like a bee in her Mancunian hive, until her last conversation got confrontational.

April was tall for a woman but red-haired Rachel Roberts, dressed to kill in a black cocktail dress and wearing six-inch heel, was taller, had bigger cans and more prominent front teeth.

Despite the height difference, they were staring each other down like two boxers listening to the ref's instructions.

Nobody else seemed to notice the two women apart from Cain and Vince Crane, the restaurant's head of security who had sidled over to his boss.

'My money is on April,' said Vince. 'Beanpole head shrinks don't make good scrappers. A shite bag-off too.'

'Personal experience?'

'Likes young meat. Suffers from Mrs Robinson syndrome. You want me to intervene?'

Cain watched the two women. Not sure if he agreed with Vince's fighting analysis. Bigger always had reach, height and weight advantages.

They would not find out.

The confrontation between the celebrity restauranteur and the psychiatrist was over before it ever started. They had backed down and had gone off in opposite directions. Panic over.

'Empty this place,' Cain said.

'Give us quarter of an hour to lock up — I'll walk you along the canal path,' said Vince. He lived in the city centre's trendy Northern Quarter. It was his usual practice to make sure they got back safely although occasionally he asked for a free pass. Temptation had snuck up on him when a leggy blond appeared from the party throng.

'Can you drive me home, Vince? I am all revved up and hot. I am ravenous.' Two-inch slash-your-back-to-ribbons false nails stroked Crane's arm.

'You don't mind if I give the walk home a miss tonight, Boss?'

He did and he didn't. Vince was free to play with fire if he wanted. His door control services were in demand because he combined brawn with brains. In Manchester, he was better connected than the national grid. His job was to keep the restaurant trouble free. No questions asked. No drugs. No hookers. No gangsters. No wankers. His reputation alone justified his hefty retainer.

By the time his cougar had powdered her nose, Vince had cleared the restaurant. The duo drove off in Vince's black

Range Rover. Burned rubber on the tarmac in a deliberate show of speedy ostentation.

Cain and April faced a ten-minute stroll to their city centre apartment building.

'Phew.' April.

'A long shift. Shall I take that?' Cain gestured to the award. Difficult to hold, tougher to carry.

'No. I like winning prizes.'

'Like me?'

'Like you.'

He bent down. They kissed under the moonlight. They kissed more intimately. Then he stopped. 'Why will I hate you?'

Her previous happy-go-lucky expression dropped like a lead balloon. 'Not in public.'

She charged off.

He reached out to grab her arm to stop her.

She resisted his attempt to restrain her and broke free.

They repeated the sequence several times as they approached Bridge 100, the unofficial border between Castlefield and Deansgate.

'Why will I hate you?' he asked several times. 'I adore the face off you.'

April's tears overflowed down her cheeks. 'How can I swear to God to honour and obey you if I don't tell you the truth?'

'About what?'

'Everything. You know so little about me. I am not a nice person.'

'That's ridiculous.'

'You must know the truth.'

'There's no such thing as the truth. Truth is just about your own perception of what you think you can and cannot see,' said Cain, realising it was the wrong time to get cod-psychological.

'Stop being silly. I am serious,' said April.

'We don't have any secrets.'

'I do. We do. Pretend we don't but we do.'

'Like what?'

'You think Ted Blake drove that car. But he didn't,' said April, as she turned her face away from him.

He closed his eyes. How did she know about Ted Blake's involvement. And how dare she claim it wasn't him?

He was hit. The impact him threw him backwards.

He felt himself fall out of control. Knew his body was going to crash. Knew could not defy gravity and was going to get hurt.

Was this how Little Miss Red Dress felt?

He expected cold hard concrete; instead, he splashed like a sack of spuds.

The air burst out of his lungs. He was having another heart attack. This one he would not survive. He waited, suspended in time.

Soon his life's highlights would flash before him. Except it never happened.

He heard raw Mancunian vomited in April's direction. 'Don't cross that line, bitch, or you're dog meat.'

Cain shouted at them. 'Leave her alone.' He thrashed through the dirty brown water to get to the side of the canal. Clawed at the canal's brick wall for leverage. Adrenalin surged through him. He screamed for more strength. 'Noooooooo.'

Two faces towered above him. One had a long scar

running from ear to ear, creating a chilling half moon smile. The youth next to him was more terrifying. In the same way Cain Bell struggled to describe April's beauty, it was impossible to find the words to describe the hatred. Was that a Nazi logo on his right cheek?

'Yum, yum scum,' sneered Swastika Boy.

'We done?' asked his friend with the man-made extended grin.

Before Swastika Boy could reply, a slurred voice screamed from the other side of the waterway. 'Gerraway or I'll smack you into next week, you yellow bastards.'

The distracted thugs looked across the canal. Cain grabbed a metal post. Heaved as hard as he could. He had traction. He could climb. Swastika Boy looked back down. Placed his palm into Cain's face. Kicked his hands until he let the bar go. Pushed him back into the water. His splash echoed with another. Somebody else was in the water.

'I am cramping up,' Cain said silently to himself as he went under. At least he thought he said it silently. He may have shouted. He surfaced and spewed muddy water. Looked up at Swastika Boy, who continued to sneer down.

'Dog meat. You too, monkey spanker.' Contempt replaced his sneer. Swastika Boy lifted his hand. Imitated a pistol. Drilled one through Cain's head. Raised the long barrel to his mouth. Blew the smoke away. He paused. Struck a tough man's pose. Then he casually headed towards Bridge 100.

Cain was out of the water and alongside April. She scrambled on the floor. Gathered up the contents of her handbag. She appeared to be unharmed apart from a bump on her temple. 'Were we mugged?' asked Cain. 'Have the bastards pinched the cash?'

'You OK, love? Did you lose consciousness?' asked their pint-sized soaked hero. He gave Cain a large brown envelope. Answered the question about the night's takings.

April nodded her head to indicate she was fine. Their red-eyed rescuer was missing a front tooth. 'How many fingers do you see?'

'Three,' she said, after a slight delay.

'You sure you didn't lose consciousness?' he asked.

She smiled half a crooked smile. 'Just want to go home.'

'What happened?' he asked her. 'My name is Nick.'

'Fell in the confusion. Might have banged my head,' said April.

'Why did they attack you?' asked Cain. He glanced at Nicks. Up close the soaked hero looked familiar, but he could not place the face. 'I'll call the police? Give me your phone.'

'No police,' said April. 'Take me home.'

'Did you know either of them? They seemed to know you,' asked Cain.

'Never seen either of them before,' she said.

He knew she was fibbing, 'How do you know about Ted Blake?' He looked at her for clues. There weren't any.

'Where do you live, Nick?' she asked.

Nick nodded to the dark side of the canal in the shadow of their skyscraper. Cain had passed the camp many times to and from work. 'She should go to A&E. Her mince pies have that glazed look when your grey matter has been scrambled too much.'

Cain could see Nick was concerned about her eyes, but he didn't know the full facts. They didn't look right because she was blind in one.

She kept that disability from the world; said she did not want anyone's pity.

Same as he had kept his visions of dead Little Miss Red Dress secret.

He trusted her more than anyone else in the universe. He looked at her and wanted to hold her, but she shrugged him away when he tried to put his left arm around her shoulders.

He loved her.

She was the most beautiful woman in the world, the dog's bollocks if you excused his French.

He was going to marry her. Spend the rest of their lives together in perfect harmony. Nothing was going to stop them.

Nobody was going to interfere in their love. Nobody was going to ruin their perfect love story, least of all her.

Three.

April disappeared into their master bedroom as soon as they entered the apartment. He would have to wait. Much as he wanted immediate answers, it was bad form to kick out a guest who had rescued them from a beating.

'April — supper for Nick?' No answer. He parked the attack. Focused on thanking Nick. 'Should clean ourselves up. We stink. Nobody does scummy canals like Manchester,' he joked.

The two of them stripped naked. He gathered their wet clothes. Shoved them in the washer. The machine clicked into action. Cain grabbed giant-sized beach towels from the airing cupboard. Wrapped one around his midriff. Handed the other to Nick.

They slowly circled each other in the spacious kitchen.

Cain glanced over at him. A muscular heavily tattooed frame the envy of men half his age. On his back a raging green Thor held aloft a huge hammer. The bell rang. There was a living boxing legend in his kitchen. 'You're Nick 'Boom-Boom' Forti?'

'I was.'

'Now?'

'Just another drunk dossing on concrete.'

'Won a few quid on you.'

'Everybody won, except me.'

'Never knew when to give up.'

'More fool me,' said Nick. 'Paid for it now.'

Cain pictured boxing nights. Posh tables with starched white tablecloths. Diners feasted on five courses while boxers punched the crap out of each other for beer money. Claret splashed on white dress shirts and surgically enhanced cleavages. The audience roared for more blood. He'd seen Nick fight at the Willows twice, long bruising battles heading for points decisions until his 'Boom-Boom' knocked his opponents out cold with one arrow. 'We can't thank you enough for helping,' said Cain.

'You'd have done it for me.'

'Of course,' said Cain. 'How did you end up..?'

'Roaming knob syndrome. She kept the house and the kid … took everything except my habit for drink.'

'We should reward you for your troubles,' said Cain, one eye on Nick's inked inky torso, the other on the cash takings April had dumped on the table. 'How much? Don't know the going rate for a hero?'

'Honest Nick should have been my fighter name. Not 'Boom-Boom'. A bottle if you want to thank me. Help me sleep. How long will my clobber take in the washer?'

'Still an hour.'

'Should shoot. Take her to hospital.'

'Stay a little longer,' said Cain. Although he was eager to let him go, he also had the undivided attention of a genuine boxing hero. Cain wanted to ask him how a lightweight could pack such brutal power? Was it anger or sheer technique?

He wanted to find out, but they had to get dressed first.

Cain stepped into the gym next to the kitchen. Grabbed sports clothes, shorts and track suit tops. Threw them at Nick. 'My boxing hero is Sonny Liston. Scariest boxer in the universe until he met Ali. My favourite boxing quote is his: someday they'll write a blues song just for fighters. It'll be for a slow guitar, soft trump and a bell. That's some epitaph for pugilists.'

Nick laughed. 'Don't fall for hard man mythology. Liston was a bully. In his defence, he died the day he was born.'

'Think he dived in the Ali fights?' asked Cain.

'Everyone has a price.'

'Did you?'

'No, too stupid. Besides, the fighting instinct takes over.'

'How do you mean?'

'Once told Iron Mike everyone has a plan until they get punched in the mouth. Until you get hurt, you don't know what you'll do,' said Nick.

'Did you meet him?'

'Once or twice. Pinched my best line. I say it now, and everyone thinks I am half inching Iron Mike's words. At leaset happier than he was.'

'Have you found peace, Nick?'

'You my bloody shrink? Don't need to be best mates just because I did what anyone would have done,' said Nick. 'Call the police. Them savages need locking up.'

'Won't be bothering the police. Just a petty tiff over pavement rights,' said Cain. 'Vince will sort it out.' He would call him in the morning. Vince would check the

CCTV footage from around the Basin. Talk to his bouncer union mates. Manchester was not awash with juvenile delinquents with facial Nazi insignia.

'Hate Dibble,' said Nick. 'They discriminate against blacks or drunks. Double shit when you're both.'

'Help yourself to anything in the drinks cabinet. Close the door on your way out,' said Cain.

He moved towards the corridor. Waited while he composed himself. Inhaled to relax himself. Finally, he heard the front door close. They were finally alone. He entered the bedroom. 'Nick's gone. What's going on? No bullshit.'

He was talking to any empty room. He was still alone. He knocked on the en suite door. Didn't want to intrude on her privacy.

There was no answer.

He gently pushed the mirrored door. It barely moved. There was an obstruction.

He pushed again.

Harder, with more conviction. Managed to shift the door. Until it was slightly ajar.

Through the crack, he peered into the bathroom. Saw her out cold. Undressed. Spread eagled on the tiled floor. Her lips were a deathly ghoulish blue. 'How long have you been lying there?'

Four.

Cain's mind was as blank as the day he was born. His bare feet frozen to the marble floor. He could not make any sense of seeing the most beautiful woman in the world motionless. In the nude. He tried to yell for help. Called her name out loud. His lips and tongue moved, but he heard no sound. Apart from a primal scream of a howling wolf hiding in the bathroom. It was so loud he covered his ears with his hands. Everyone had a plan until they were punched in the mush.

'What's up?' asked Nick Forti. He had burst into the spacious bathroom.

'She's dead.'

'You checked?'

'Seen dead people before.'

'How do you know?'

'Lips are blue. She's a ghost already.'

'Call an ambulance. Now,' shouted Nick.

'What you going to do?'

'Make the call. Give me your towel.' Cain whipped off his towel from his waist. Started to cover April's naked body. 'A pillow. We've all seen naked women, mate. I am an alcoholic. Not a rapist. Phone.'

'Is she alive?'

Nick sank to his knees. Shook April gently to see if she would wake. Grabbed a shaving mirror. Held it under her nose. 'Blue lips mean lack of oxygen. She's not breathing,' said Nick. He rolled her onto her back. Tilted her head to clear her airwaves. Rested it on the makeshift pillow. 'Call an ambulance.'

Cain couldn't move. Nick jumped up. Slapped his face.

'You're in shock. Please call.'

The slap cleared Cain's head. He sprang into action. His mobile was ruined from the fall in the canal. He would use the landline. He stopped as he watched Nick place his hand on April's flattened breasts. 'You done this before?'

'I've watched TV,' said Nick. He pumped hard on her chest.

'Don't break her ribs.'

'Least of her worries. Ambulance.'

Ten minutes later, a paramedic, armed with a mobile defibrillator, relieved Nick.

'What happened?' asked another paramedic, who keyed info into a tablet.

'Found her unconscious on the bathroom floor,' said Cain.

'Did she bang her head in here or outside?'

'I don't know.'

'How long was she unconscious?'

'I don't know. I don't know anything.'

'Is she on any medication?'

'No.'

'Any health conditions? Heart disease? Diabetes? High blood pressure?'

'No. Blind in one eye. Apart from that …'

'We'll take her to A&E soon as we can stabilise her.'

'Is she going to be OK?' The paramedic didn't answer as she issued fresh instructions to her colleagues.

In the kitchen, Nick Forti poured chilled Oliver's 9.4 ABV Herefordshire cider. 'Thank you,' said Cain. 'Owe you big time.'

'No worries. Hope she makes it.'

An ambulance blue-lighted April to North Manchester General Hospital's A&E department in Crumpsall. Cain had left Nick clutching another cider. Should have asked him to stay. Guard the flat with the smashed front door. But it had slipped his mind. Nick could take what he wanted. Anyone could. Small price to pay for saving his fiancée's life. He grimaced at his cynical fatalism. Was Nick a thief just because he was a homeless alcoholic? Why did he always think the worst of good people and hero worship thugs like Sonny Liston? He knew — he was contaminated by low expectations and transparent self-interest. Only haters hated. His one saving grace, he knew his faults. Cynicism ran through him like the letters in sticks of Blackpool rock.

A team of doctors and nurses were waiting when they arrived.

They took over from the paramedics. Pushed April on a trolley into a side room off the main corridor. They exuded calm; Cain's heart beat faster than John Bonham's drumming intro to Led Zeppelin's 'Rock'n'Roll'.

A nurse showed him into a waiting room. Introduced herself as staff nurse Frankie Moore. Asked questions about medication and pre-existing health conditions. Same as the paramedics had fired at him. He gave her the same answers back and how the blindness in one eye meant he was always the designated driver.

'Talking about designating, are you April's designated decision maker?' He nodded. They were partners in the Red Manifesto and in life. 'We'll need proof but not tonight.'

'Why?'

'Standard procedure for admissions with life threatening injuries unable to make decisions.'

'We got engaged tonight. She will be able to walk down the aisle, won't she?'

'So you're not the next of kin? Does she have family, children?'

'Yes. A daughter, I've never met her.'

'Do you know her name?'

'Summer. Never been introduced. April was married to Bob Ord, you know the Hollywood film producer.'

'Do you have an agreement for circumstances like this?' asked Frankie. 'Sorry, if I appear insensitive.'

'She wanted to marry me. Not die…' He stopped himself. No prizes for being an arsehole in front of a nurse who was only trying to do her job. 'Is she going to be OK?'

'Do you have the daughter's contact details?'

'No,' he said and he didn't. Whenever he mentioned her daughter or her ex-husband April stonewalled him. Told him they lived in the present, not the past.

'Anyone you want to call? Shouldn't be alone in a situation like this.' Frankie's brown eyes were full of pity for him and he hated it.

'Alone, I am not alone,' said Cain to himself after she had

left the room. Little Miss Red Dress was sat opposite him, her legs barely reached the floor.

'Daddy, don't cry.'

'I won't darling,' said Cain. 'She said she knows about Ted Blake, but said he wasn't driving the car that hit you. How would she know that? And why? Only four people knew. Ted, Len, me and you. You and Ted are floating in a most peculiar way amongst the stars. So how would she know?'

'I don't know, Daddy.'

'So who was it who broke your neck if it wasn't Ted Blake? Do you know? Did you see him?' She never answered. She had gone again. Like she had done so many times before. Not that she would know the answer. Cain would have to wait until April was able to talk.

Frankie Moore was back in the room with a heavyweight sumo wrestler dressed in tight green scrubs. They were about to tell him she was OK.

Whatever doubts she had by the canal, they could work them out when she was better.

As soon as she was able to talk, they could go back to normal and start making serious wedding plans.

Five.

A time-served journalist turned public relations guru, Cain Bell instinctively took the initiative. He was up on his feet and had shaken hands with Frankie and her colleague before the door had shut. 'Can I see her?' he asked. 'Has she been asking for me?'

'This is neurosurgeon Raj Ghandi. Raj, this is Cain Bell, April's business and life partner. They got engaged yesterday evening,' said Frankie.

'Congratulations. Tonight you gave her the best possible wedding present. Your prompt actions saved her life,' said Raj. 'Are you the next of kin?'

'Not sure what that means,' said Cain.

'It's OK, Raj,' interrupted Frankie. 'Her daughter Summer is happy to include him.'

'Is she OK?'

'April has an acute subdural haematoma,' said Raj, 'a blood clot between the brain's surface and outer covering.'

'Is it serious?' asked Cain, regretting never paying attention to school biology lessons beyond reproduction.

'We must do a craniotomy to stop the bleeding.'

'What are the odds …?' Cain stopped mid-sentence as he realised the stupidity of his question. His heart attack had been simple. April had performed CPR. He had been rushed to A&E. They had installed two stents. He had changed his lifestyle. Nobody had entered his head. Messed with his brains.

'We rely on science,' said Raj. He left the room.

Frankie remained. 'Raj is a brilliant surgeon. April could not be in better hands. I've also spoken to April's daughter,' said Frankie. 'She is driving with her father from the Wirral tonight.'

'April's my partner…do I get a say?'

'It is up to her next of kin.'

'But if she is marrying me?'

'I cannot advise you, I am afraid. I am just a humble staff nurse,' said Frankie. 'When I spoke to her she was happy to share updates with you.'

'That's very kind of her,' said Cain.

'The police are outside. They want a word about the attack.'

They entered the room dressed in heavy-duty body-armour. The two uniformed officers, one male and one female, introduced themselves. One was Charlie, the other George.

They started with a few easy questions. Classic what, when, where and speculative whys before they got down to the nitty gritty. 'Have you been drinking, Cain?'

'I'd proposed. She'd accepted. We were celebrating.' Cain instinctively distrusted authority. The next question confirmed he was right to be cautious.

'How many?'

'Two glasses of Chablis, possibly three. Three Perrier waters. Why the interest? You won't catch them asking me about my drinking habits.'

'We approach serious assaults with an open mind.'

Cain tried to remain calm. 'Psychopaths with a swastika tattoo and ear-to-ear scars are the knobs you should be chasing, not me.'

'We've alerted the patrols in the area,' said the WPC. 'Did you know two-thirds of women are murdered by a partner or a former partner. How come your knuckles are grazed?'

'Climbing out of a canal. I am the victim, not the criminal here. I didn't hit her.'

'If she dies this could be murder investigated by detectives twice as bright as us. The paramedics said you were naked when they arrived?'

'And?'

'Had you been fighting in bed? The front door smashed down. Were you engaged in a game that got out of hand?'

The male officer appeared to be embarrassed. 'We have to follow every possible line of enquiry. Sorry.'

'I fell in the canal. A homeless man rescued us. She had been knocked out by two thugs. One with a Nazi tattoo. The other scarred from ear to ear. We were wet and cold and stank. We went to our apartment to recuperate and wash our clothes. I found April unconscious on the floor. That's it.'

'Who was the third man — your rescuer?' asked the WPC.

'George?' said the male officer, trying to grab the WPC's attention.

'Nick Forti.'

'The boxer? Where is he now?' asked the WPC.

'George, let me handle this,' said Charlie. 'Your attackers. One had a swastika under his right eye, a bit like a teardrop?' The male officer pointed to his own face. Cain nodded. 'The other man, the one of the big smiley face. Was his face scarred?' The officer extended his own mouth on either. 'Looks like an extended grin?'

Cain nodded again. 'Yes.'

'Give us a couple of seconds.'

The male officer took the WPC aside. When they returned, the mood had changed. There was only one reason for the change in attitude. They had recognised their attackers.

'I am stepping outside to make a call,' said the WPC. She left the room, leaving Cain with Charlie. When the officer returned, she handed Cain a mobile. 'Rita Rock wants a word.'

'Rita Rock here, I am a serious crimes detective. Very sorry to hear about your partner's situation. PC Golding described your attackers to me. I'd like to do a formal ID as quickly as possible.'

'Am I in danger?'

'No, but I've ordered the two officers to stay with you until I arrive. Don't leave the hospital or speak to anyone under any circumstances. See you soon.'

Six.

The two officers stood guard outside the waiting room. Left Cain by himself. One day the threesome allegations would be a great anecdote if they fixed April. He should complain about their attitude, but he knew he wouldn't.

Life was too short to pick unnecessary fights.

Rita Rock had told him not to contact anyone so he wanted to do the opposite.

He thought about calling friends to sit with him, but it wasn't fair to ask them to share his raw grief.

Most people were uncomfortable when exposed to tragedy. He'd been there before and knew exactly how everyone would react.

The door opened and the male police officer entered cautiously.

Behind him was a woman dressed in jeans and a white jumper, an overlarge silver cross around her neck. Rita Rock moved exceptionally fast, thought Cain, unless she already at the hospital.

'This is Summer,' said the uniformed officer.

A spit of his fiancée breezed past the policeman. 'You must be Cain. Took my breath away when the nurse said you were her fiancé.'

'I only proposed tonight. Took myself by surprise.'

'How exciting. Do you mind if we wait here with you? The old man will be here shortly.'

Cain nodded for her to join him. 'Be my guest.'

'Drove over soon as we were called. The old man's getting coffees. Do you want anything?'

'No thanks,' said Cain.

'Never driven so fast in my life?' Cain noticed she spoke like all young people, where a statement automatically became a question. 'Is it serious?'

'Serious as it gets.'

'We should pray. Join me. Follow me.' She clasped her hands. Opened her eyes wide. Raised her head to the skies. Her voice was soft, gentle and soothing, pillow talk, seducing the non-existent Big Guy upstairs.

> *O Holy Spirit please come like a dove*
> *Shield and protect now the one that I love.*
> *Cover her wounds with your grace feathered wings,*
> *Shield her from sorrow, breathe hope songs within.*
> *Tend with your goodness the pain that she bears*
> *Heal now her injuries with miracle care.*
> *Carry her high far above till they see*
> *Your rainbow of promise, real hope lies ahead.*
> *I love her so dearly, so help me to be all that you, Jesus, would give out through me.*
> *Amen*

'Amen,' mumbled Cain, embarrassed at participating in an imaginary conversation with a man-made control mechanism. Why was it so difficult to tell people with faith that you were an atheist? Religious people had no problem offending non-believers.

'Rushed here soon as we heard from that lovely Scottish nurse. Lucky we were at home. We're working on a couple of big film projects, one here in the UK and the other in the USA. Could easily have been state-side.'

'You're welcome to stay at our flat,' said Cain.

'You're too kind. What happened?' asked Summer.

Before Cain had a chance to respond the door opened again.

The police officer introduced Bob Ord and ushered in a stooped living film legend deep into his sixties or early seventies.

He wore an idiosyncratic combination of beige biscuit suit, flower power shirt and purple DMs.

In his hands he carried three takeaway Costa coffee cups encased in a cardboard tray.

'Is this April's toy boy, Summer?'

As opposed to her sugar daddy, thought Cain, although he kept his reply to himself. Bob Ord was clearly used to saying whatever came into his head. Celebrity and fame had made him oblivious to social niceties.

'Cain, my dad is all bluster. His bark is worse than his bite.'

'As a daughter, she is shite at public relations, even with God watching her back. She only does it to please the mad WASPY Americans in Hollyweird. Very convincing acting. And sadly necessary in this day and age.'

'Pleased to meet you, Bob,' said Cain.

'Tell me what happened,' said Bob.

They both listened to the edited highlights. Summer clutched her cross tight. Bob nursed his coffee like a chalice. Cain deliberately missed out Ted Blake, the words uttered by Swastika Boy and the descriptions of his assailants.

When he had finished Bob reacted with a short laugh. 'Tell me what really happened? Fell over pissed? Too much weed? You weren't poking her, and she fell off the bed. A young buck with your stature. You know what they say about men with big feet? A real liberated wild child was my April. Unlike Summer here, waiting for Mr Right.'

'Pops, not everyone shares your wicked sense of humour. He lives his life without rules because he's rich and famous. I do apologise for my father. His middle name is Insensitivity.'

'Thanks for the personal reference, SummerBabe, not that I need one with a sideboard full of awards' said Bob. 'Not pissing my pants, sweetheart? The old sword is in fine upstanding fettle.'

'Soon as you do, we'll book you into a care home for aged film producers.'

'Can't wait. Least I'll get some respect from my peers. They will appreciate me.'

Cain felt slightly jealous at their apparent closeness.

'Seriously, she's going to be OK?' asked Bob.

'Her heart stopped. She wasn't breathing,' said Cain.

'She's a survivor. She's faced worse. Much worse.'

'Worse than almost dying?' asked Cain.

Bob ignored him. Sipped his coffee. Checked his watch.

After the initial nervous chat, the long wait began. They studied their mobile devices.

Normally Cain would have loved access to a world-famous film producer. Like he could have chewed the fat with Nick Forti while they riffed on pugilism. Nick would have hundreds of stories, just like Bob. Cain loved classic Taylor-era Stones before they became a heritage act. He would have loved to ask Bob what Jagger and Richards thought about being played by Manchester scallies with mockney accents and bad skin.

But it wasn't the right time to be a fan. Not when the woman they loved was fighting for her life.

When Summer left to visit the ladies, Bob sidled over to Cain. 'Between you and me, no need to involve the police. They'll only get a slap on the wrist. Friends owe me a few favours. Mum's the word.'

Bob was back in his chair by the time Summer returned with Raj and Frankie.

Were they here to deliver good or bad news? Cain could not tell from their poker-faces.

She was bound to be OK. His karma was good. He did good deeds. Supported Greenpeace and Amnesty. Was a forty-quid-a-year humanist.

There was no way he deserved to be prematurely bereaved twice in his life before he was fifty.

Seven.

Raj introduced himself to the newcomers. Invited everyone to sit down. Suggested they sat in a small circle so they didn't raise their voices.

Although he exuded calmness, Cain thought he must have been exhausted. Putting your hands inside a human's head and rearranging complex grey blancmange circuitry had to be pretty stressful. One minuscule mistake would have major, if not fatal, consequences.

'We've stopped the bleed on the brain. That's the good news. She is now in a medically induced coma. We've lowered her body temperature. We're going to keep her between thirty-four and thirty-five degrees Celsius while her brain is at its most inflamed. Think of it as cooling a car engine down so we can allow the healing process to occur without April losing too many brain cells.'

'Is she fucked?' asked Bob Ord. 'A cabbage?'

Cain grimaced at April's estranged husband's starkness. Raj, presumably, had heard it all before because he didn't flinch.

'One challenge at a time, Mr Ord. We don't speculate beyond the evidence we see. At the moment, there is no brain activity on our scans, but that could be down to the drugs she is on. Worst case? I'll be honest with you. She is either brain dead, because the brain stem no longer functions, or she remains in a permanently persistent vegetative state, as you suggested, with no cognitive or mental activity until she dies.'

'Dies?' asked Summer.

'Death is inevitable in that situation,' said Raj.

'Is there any hope?'

'Of course, she might make a full recovery,' said Raj. 'It will take time, I am afraid to say, but we will give her our full and undivided attention.'

'Is she in pain?' Cain asked.

'As I said, she's in an induced coma. She won't be aware of anything,' said Raj. 'You might be faced with making some big decisions if we know for certain there is no brain stem activity. If we have the worst-case scenario, would, for example, April want to offer her organs for transplant?'

'Is this the right time to discuss transplants?' asked Cain, thinking if he had he ever seen April with a donor card?

'April would want her organs used. I believe there are strict deadlines, so you have to move quick otherwise they start to rot and are unusable,' said Summer.

'Do I have a say?' asked Cain.

'No offence, old chap. But you're only involved in this discussion as a courtesy to Summer,' said Bob. 'She's a Christian who believes the Good Samaritan is a true story. Same with the fish and the bread. Feeding the five thousand. She sees good in all of us. Even me.'

'You can't be the next of kin?' asked Cain. 'You're divorced aren't you?'

'Summer is the next of kin. Although she will always ask for my advice. Her old dad knows what is best.'

Cain looked towards the young woman. She half-smiled in her confusion. Repeated her earlier question. 'She's not going to die?'

'We don't know. I'll let you see her for five minutes. I'd recommend you go home and freshen up. She's going to be in a coma for at least two days,' said Raj. 'If the situation changes, we'll contact you immediately.'

'Thank you,' said Summer.

'Thank you,' said Cain.

They trooped together into the ICU unit. Frankie led them to the bed.

Cain thought she still looked beautiful. Wires monitored what he assumed were her blood pressure, heart rate and blood oxygen levels. Bodies were remarkable machines. So resilient and yet so easily damaged. He wanted time alone with his sleeping beauty. 'Would you mind if I had a minute?'

'I'll pray outside,' said Summer. 'Are you going to say a prayer too, we'll be stronger together? My old man is teasing. I take my faith very seriously.'

'I just want a word in private,' said Cain. Alone, apart from the nursing and medical staff, he sat down and whispered:

You've got to pull through this, April. You cannot leave me here by myself. Not without any warning. We've got to get old together, disgracefully. You can't just decide to jump ship when I've planned the prefect wedding.

34

And you are going to walk down the aisle with me.

I am going to book the Manchester Art Gallery for our marriage. Will be a really stunning venue, as you know. You'll adore it. I know you will.

We'll get married amongst the paintings in the English & French impressionist's gallery. .

I've got an invite list of a hundred and twenty friends and family who can share our really special day. Have to add your daughter to the list. She's a nice girl. Reminds me of my Hannah. If she had lived.

I've not picked my best man yet. I am not telling you who it is. It will spoil the surprise. Ditto the honeymoon. All I can say is you'll adore the Mediterranean location.

It's going to cost but you're worth every penny. Every single one. I need you to stay with me. I know you think I'd hate you, but I am sure you have a valid explanation for those secrets. Just poor timing to mention it today.

It is what it is.

We'll sort it out when you're better. Fight for me. Fight for Summer. Stay with me. Stay with us. There's no leaving now or ever.

A tear dropped from his eyes onto the bed frame. He got up carefully from the chair. Two women were waiting in the wings, their faces hidden in a half-light halo around their heads. 'Hello Cain, I am Rita Rock. Can we talk in private?'

Eight.

Rita Rock brought over machine coffee ming to the table in the near deserted hospital restaurant. A couple of night staff nibbled at homemade sandwiches. Sipped from flasks in graveyard shift isolation, oblivious to the detective and the PR man. She sat herself down at the table and looked like she hadn't slept for 48 hours.

On the phone she had sounded young. In person she had large bags under tired eyes. Her skin cried out for moisturiser to soften the wrinkles. But beyond Rita's knackered mug, her eyes were buzzing. This case excited her, much as she tried to disguise her adrenalin.

She nonchalantly handed Cain her business card with a handwritten mobile number scribbled on the front. The card stated her rank as detective inspector.

'Last DI I spoke to was called Len Harvey. You're too young to remember him,' said Cain.

'Flattery gets you everywhere,' she smiled. 'I am old enough to remember dear old Lenny. I worked with him early-doors. How do you know him?'

'He was leading an investigation way back in the day. Would be nice to catch up with him,' said Cain. Would be great to ask him how April knew about Ted Blake if only two people had heard his confession before he died.

'I'll ask around the office, see if I can find out where he is now. Shall we get down to business? If you feel this is not the right time, just say.'

'No, it is fine,' he said.

'You're happy to have an informal chat while the attack is still fresh in your mind?'

Cain nodded his agreement. Although Bob was against involving the police, he wanted to hear what the detective had to say. If she could give him a couple of names, it would save Vince Crane time in the morning. He was curious about one thing.

'Why the rush? We don't normally get this speedy service,' he said. He already knew the answer because of the reaction of the two uniforms to the descriptions of their assailants.

She ignored his question. 'We will do a formal statement soon, but in your own words, what happened?' She opened a note pad and took notes while he spoke. He repeated the story he had told the two officers. Missed out the words about a bitch crossing a line and ending up as dog meat. Told her something was said, but he could not hear it.

She asked him again and he repeated he was not even able to hazard a guess. He didn't want to grass April up by mistake.

Rita stopped taking notes. Flipped the notebook shut. Sucked on the top of the pen. 'This is off the record. A good defence lawyer will claim she banged her head against the bath, the sink, toilet or bidet when she fell in the bathroom.'

'You're joking?'

'Strictly between you and me, it throws up reasonable doubt unless we can prove the assailant knocked April unconscious.'

'How do you do that?'

'We'll check CCTV footage from the area. See if we can identify the two people you describe in the vicinity of locks 92 and 93 on the Rochdale Canal at the times you've indicated. We'll also do an appeal for witnesses. Arrange for A-boards to be placed on the canal towpath to jog memories. Castlefield is a popular destination. There are bound to be people who saw or heard the assault. We'll try and get corroborative evidence, but yours is crucial.'

'It is?'

'You tell me she was unconscious. And you identify your attackers so we can arrest and interview them. Check these out.'

'OK.' She opened her iPad. Swiped through a few pages. Presented the device to Cain. Sat close next to him so they could both see the pictures. He zapped through dozens of mugshots. After he had shaken his head at each picture, she thanked him. 'I am sorry,' he said.

'Shall we go through them again. I'll swipe. You watch.'

Cain watched her fingers work the screen. She wore cracked red nail varnish over bitten nails. There were faint nicotine stains on the index and middle fingers of her right hand. Once that sort of thing had been romantic in his youth. Now it looked slightly seedy and unkempt.

Her fingers slowed down. Paused over a face without any tattoos. A young face that looked incredibly familiar. Swastika Boy before he defaced himself. She left the image there. 'If you identity him, they won't be able to get to you. I swear on the lives of my children. Once you've told me, we'll make sure you're protected one hundred percent. If you see him, just touch the screen.'

'Go on. We'll go through a third time,' said Cain.

He was unsure about the pros and cons of pointing the finger at Swastika Boy.

Would the magistrates refuse him bail? Put him on remand. That was great in theory. But if they let him, bailed him, he was dog meat.

Cain didn't know how many children Rita had, but she wasn't going to sacrifice them for him, no matter how well intentioned she wanted to appear.

Don't tell the police. That was the message from Bob Ord and just about every journalist Cain knew since he had learned shorthand during the bum fluff years.

'Some more friendly advice off the record, Cain. This is me as Rita, your friend. It's perfectly normal to be scared after a vicious attack, especially when the consequences are potentially so severe and life threatening.'

'I know,' said Cain, unsure how they'd become buddies after quarter of an hour's chat over tepid machine coffee. Then again, he had invited Summer and Bob to stay at his apartment in city centre Manchester in the same time frame. They were waiting for him now.

'Police officers are far more likely to be hurt than civilians like you.'

'The contrary evidence …is lying in intensive care…'

'That's bad luck. Manchester is blighted by criminal gangs and rotten families who allow their children to run riot around the city. They condone their violence and cover up their crimes. Build invisible but effective walls of silence. Scare good people like you. But if you fight back, we can all fight back. Together, we can make that wall fall, but you need to pull the first brick out,' said Rita Rock.

She opened her iPad again and up came some more mugshots of older men. 'Whoever did this is dangerous and needs to be taken off the streets.'

Cain spotted Swastika Boy's grinning accomplice immediately.

He tapped the iPad screen. 'That could be one of them,' he said.

'And the one you paused over on the previous set?'

'Could be.'

'Yes or no?'

'If I said yes, who are they?' asked Cain.

'I am not at liberty to tell you.'

Cain smiled at her. Felt exhausted and stimulated at the same time. Could understand why she felt the same way. 'You want me to say yes, I want to know what I am getting myself into here?'

'Can't do that,' she said.

'OK. I cannot recognise anyone,' said Cain and stood up. 'Thanks for the coffee.' Watched her work out if it was worth compromising her integrity.

'Swear blind, this stays strictly between you and me. You promise?'

'I do.'

'On your own children's life?'

'Yes,' said Cain, not in the mood to split hairs with the detective about the validity of the oath if the child was already dead.

'The tattooed young man is Ryan McGinty. Scarface is Liam 'Two Smiles' Devine. They are the son and brother-in-law of Billy McGinty. You've heard of Billy McGinty, haven't you?'

Cain nodded. 'Who hasn't heard of Billy McGinty. I try to avoid his sort.'

'Ever met him?'

'Not that I am aware.'

'Never visited the restaurant?'

'Our paths have never crossed and we spend a fortune on security keeping it that way.'

'Not his people?'

'Crane Door Control. Vince Crane heads it.'

'So you've never had any contact with Billy or his family?'

'No.'

'What about April? Does she know him?' asked Rita.

That was a good question, thought Cain. Why would she know Billy McGinty?

Nine.

Cain had a name, McGinty. Or three names to be accurate, Ryan, Liam and Billy. He also had two house guests.

He wanted to ask them if April knew the McGinty clan even if that compromised his pact with Rita Rock.

He wanted to ask Bob if he knew Ted Blake, rock and roll roadie.

Forget his own pact with Len Harvey. The sell-by date on that deal expired when Harvey hung up his handcuffs.

He knew that was why he offered to put Bob and Summer up. Rainy city was awash with hotel rooms and they had plenty of cash. But you cannot interrogate from a distance. Impossible.

You needed constant access to chip away at their defensive walls without them realising you were messing with the brickwork. They were not going to volunteer any incriminating information. What was the line April should not cross? A simple question was as explosive as a cup of undiluted nitroglycerin.

Outside the hospital Summer and Bob beelined to the

disabled car park across the road from the hospital's main entrance.

They zapped a black range rover with a BOB1 number plate and a blue badge on the dash.

He expected Bob to drive and Summer to jump into the passenger seat, but they reversed gender stereotypes. 'Who has the disability ..?' asked Cain.

'Dad has epilepsy,' said Summer.

'Does that disqualify you from driving? April can legally drive but doesn't feel safe with just the one good eye...' said Cain. He climbed into the back.

'Never knew mum had eye problems,' said Summer.

'Detached retina. Before you were born,' said Bob.

Summer pulled the Range Rover out of the hospital. Cain gave her directions to head back into the city centre. 'Turn left, and then first right. We'll go down Leicester Road.'

'That ghetto still full of them Jews? Or has them Muslims wiped them out?' asked Bob. He didn't wait for an answer. Turned his attention to his daughter. 'Your mum never wanted anybody's pity. She's like me. Her eye. My epilepsy. Drugs control my condition, but they cannot guarantee I am ever going to be seizure-free. Would never be able to live with myself if I blacked out and had a fatal accident.'

'April said the same thing about her sight. Couldn't live with it on her conscience,' said Cain, thinking most people couldn't, except the late Ted Blake.

'What happened to Boddingtons?' asked Bob. He glanced to his left as Summer navigated through Bury New Road's fast fashion wholesale district.

'They killed the Cream of Manchester when they sold out to a bigger brewer,' said Cain. 'The old brewery is a car park. Must have driven the prisoners crazy. All those wonderful malty, hoppy smells wafting in through metal bars on a brewday.'

Summer pulled up at the traffic lights across the junction from the Manchester Arena and Victoria station.

A radicalised youth blew himself up at an Ariane Grande concert six months earlier; took twenty-two innocent young lives with him. Maimed and tortured a whole lot more.

Cain refused to use the terrorist's name out of respect for the slaughtered.

'I hope Salman Abedi is rotting in hell, getting pegged every time he draws breath. Summer's God preaches forgiveness, but I want an eye for eye,' said Bob. 'I reckon this city is cursed, you know. Everyone knows where they were when the bomb exploded in May. Same as when the IRA blew up the city centre. Only a miracle stopped hundreds of people being killed. Not so lucky on that flight to Corfu in the eighties. Fifty-five died. Add that to the ten who were killed in Woolworths in 1979 and you begin to see a pattern. And don't forget the Busby Babes. The best footballing team in the world struck down before they'd reached their prime. These stories stick in the mind. Haunt you big time. Shipman, Brady and Hindley. The bloke who killed Massey two years previously. Best decision me and April ever made was to leave here in the nineties after we had Summer and *All Down The Line* took off. Changed my bank balance from red to black in the time it takes to click your fingers.'

'Just bad luck,' said Cain, out of instinct than belief, as the lights turned green.

They inched forward in the gridlocked city centre.

Planners were changing the shape of the city yet again and travel was down to a snail's pace. They could walk quicker. 'Wrong place, wrong time. That's all.'

'Not just the big numbers, individuals too, as we all know from personal experience. Wilson, Gretton, Hammett, Georgie Best, Summerbee, Curtis, the bloke from the Fall. All of them cursed to die young because of this city. I thought April had escaped, but you brought her back and now look what's happened. Place needs an exorcism. Can your God arrange one, Summer?'

'You may mock with your pagan ways, but the Good Lord loves you despite your cynicism.'

'Is he going to save her? Can your prayers guarantee that?' Bob asked his daughter.

Cain looked at her to assess her reaction. She blanked the question. Turned on the CD player. Another Manchester band, the Hollies, did their take on *The Air That I Breathe*. The melancholic song shut Bob up and the three of them retreated into their own worlds for the rest of the crawl home.

Twenty minutes later they were in the lift of one of the highest residential skyscrapers in the UK.

Cain thought they would be impressed as long as a drunken Nick Forti wasn't unconscious in a pool of piss.

They entered the apartment; Nick Forti wasn't there. Cain expected them to be wowed by the views of Wales, Cheshire and the city. Summer was but Bob wasn't. Cain's inner tourist guide rebelled at his indifference. 'This place was the catalyst for Manchatten.'

'Seen bigger and better,' said Bob, dismissively.

'Make yourself at home. Anything you want. Guest

rooms are permanently ready for use. We have a cleaner come in three times a week. Keys are in the rooms,' said Cain.

He was slightly confused. The apartment looked immaculate. Washed clothes were neatly folded. Cups washed. Bottles thrown away. Maybe he had got his days mixed up. The cleaner had already been. Perhaps Nick had … no he was a hapless alcoholic.

'Very trusting,' said Bob.

'We're all family. We all have April's best interests at heart,' said Cain. He noticed the cash April had discarded casually on the dining room table was neatly stacked. There was a piece of paper by it.

He walked over to have a look. A note from Nick: hope your missus is OK. Tidied the place up for you. Old soldiers never die. Chin up. 'Boom-Boom'. The handwriting was neat and tidy, like his boxing had been.

'She's not done much with the place since I was last here.'

'You been here before?' asked Cain.

'Had to approve the purchase.'

'I thought April bought it?'

'No. She chose it.'

'You're mistaken, she owns it,' said Cain.

'No. It's owned by my investment company.'

'April's never mentioned you as the owner of this property. Or a third party.'

'Maybe you weren't listening hard enough,' said Bob.

'If she dies you can make me homeless?'

'Don't jump the gun, but you're probably right with your assessment. Just hope Summer doesn't want to move to Manchester if her mum passes.'

'Sure is,' she replied as she stared out over Wales. 'It's like the Grand Canyon with houses rather than red rock and a huge river. You two must have been very happy here?'

Cain nodded. Didn't like the use of the past tense. 'I can't cook like April, but even I cannot mess up scrambled egg and smoked salmon.'

They weren't paying any attention to him, unlike April who used to always looked at you as if you were the most important person in the world.

He went to the fridge. The salad and the dressing would transform the breakfast into something special. The smoked salmon would be fine chopped from a fresh fillet. All the grub in the apartment came from the Red Manifesto. The EPOS system logged the items under food and menu development. April loved to experiment with food and recipes. Filmed herself when she cooked new things. They were an equal partnership and they loved each other unconditionally.

'Don't we love?'

He turned away from the open fridge. Expected to see April leaning on the central island in the kitchen, glass of wine in her hand and a smile wider than the Mersey.

Except she wasn't there. In that single moment, the reality of his situation kicked in.

He excused himself.

Went to the toilet and threw up. Several times until he was heaving on empty.

Looked at himself long and hard in the mirror when he had nothing left to vomit. 'Don't you dare leave me, April. Now is not the time.'

He repeated the words with less conviction each time before he changed them for a simple why you? Manchester wasn't cursed. Bob was talking bollocks about exorcisms and taking the piss out of his daughter's beliefs. He'd never have been that unkind towards Little Miss Red Dress if she had been religious. 'What did you do to upset bloody nutcase gangsters?' And what did he do when he had the answers? Lightning wasn't likely to strike twice. Ted Blake had got just what he deserved with a very painful but quick death. But Cain could not be lucky twice.

Ten.

After eating, Cain resisted the temptation to have an illuminating date with Google God. There was research to be done on the untrusted, unreliable internet, but it could wait until he felt less wired to fact find on the McGinty clan.

Instead, he tried to grab an early morning power nap. But there was a huge hole in the bed without her.

He could smell her on the bed linen; see her body shape indented on the mattress. Sleep would only make it worse.

When he woke, he would expect her next to him. Then he would remember, but for 10 seconds before he did, she would still be there, the most beautiful woman in the world, his fiancée.

He glanced at the alarm clock by the side of his bed. He had hardly blinked and it was already 8.45am.

He must have slept without realising it. The world was going to work while April fought to stay alive thanks to Billy McGinty and his family.

He would speak to both Vince and Evening News crime reporter, Matt Stark, the smoothest, coolest journalist who ever sauntered down Deansgate to the press club.

Both were more reliable sources than the internet. What was a reasonable hour to call them?

Vince would still be loved up with his bride while Matt had to get six kids ready for school. Once Matt had his morning editorial meeting he would be free.

Before he could decide, April's mobile rang. He saw a Manchester number he didn't recognise. He reached across to pick up the handset.

'Is that April, April Sands?'

'No, who's calling.'

'I recognise those sexy dulcet tones. Hi Cain, it's June Hastie. What's this I hear about bizarre sex games getting out of hand - you, April the celebrity chef and a punch-drunk boxing champ? Want to tell me about your love triangle?'

'Hi June, nice to hear from you,' said Cain.

He pictured her. A pisspot peddling click-bait bullshit. She was once an untouchable. Had eyes only for editors who could give her a quick bunk up the greasy pole. 'We're speaking off the record, aren't we?'

'Sure. My sources say you two regularly pick up the homeless for threesomes.'

'Your sources are mistaken.'

'Anything you'd like to say on the record?'

'No story here, June. April's in intensive care after brain surgery, but that's private and off the record. Me and her, off the record, were attacked by racists. If you want a story, write about the canal pusher serial killer responsible for 70 deaths in the city over two decades.'

'That's fiction. I want stories with legs.'

'Who was your source again?' asked Cain.

'A good journalist never reveals her sources?'

'But what about bad ones like me and you?'

'Still your self-deprecating self. Shall we go on the record? I am going to write something.'

'Not while she's fighting for her life.'

'Do you regularly pick up homeless men for bedroom romps?'

'Don't be crazy.'

'Nick Forti is the boxer's name I've been given. A pugilist turned rent boy?'

'April is really ill.'

'24-hours, Cain, or less, depending if the story goes live. At the moment, you're a 'no comment' from behind a closed door.'

'June, don't…' The line went dead. Bloody cat-strangler thought Cain. Pissed off by Hastie's call, he dialled the restaurant's most expensive employee.

Vince Crane answered immediately. 'Hi April. What's up?'

'It's Cain.'

'How we doing, Boss? Flat out exhausted after last night's drive home.'

'April and me were attacked.'

'Stop messing with me.'

'Deadly serious.'

'Mugged outside the restaurant? I'll knee-cap the bastards. You OK?'

'April is on life support — but that's not for public consumption, understand?'

'You're pulling my plonker, Boss. She's not badly hurt, is she?'

'Bad as it gets. Can we chat privately at the Manifesto?'

'You keeping it open?'

'Yes,' said Cain, making a mental note to call the general manager Cody James after Vince and before he chatted with Matt Stark.

'Descriptions?' asked Vince.

'White youth with a swastika tattoo. A man with a scar from ear to ear,' replied Cain, 'Any ideas?'

'I'll ask around, Boss.'

'Hope that bird was worth it? If you'd walked shotgun, the cowards wouldn't have attacked us.'

'I feel bad as it is, Boss. If anything happens, I'll never forgive myself.'

'Might have met your future wife?'

'The bride not second date material.'

Vince ended the call without deviating into football and music. Cain knew why. The descriptions would only fit two people and Vince had shown he didn't want to cross Billy McGinty.

Cain called Cody James, Red Manifesto's general manager. Kept it simple. Said April was in for observation.

'She won't be away for long, will she?' asked Cody.

'No,' said Cain. 'Carry on as normal. Pretend we're both on holiday for a fortnight. By the way, is the private dining room booked? I might bring April's ex and her daughter down for food.'

Finally, he called his drinking buddy and the local Evening Newspaper crime reporter, Matt Stark. He answered second ring. 'Hey Cain, a great night last night. You been to bed yet?'

'April's critically ill. Her bloody heart stopped.'

'What the fuck?' asked Matt. 'How is she?'

'Off the record, knocking on heaven's door,' said Cain. He told him the story.

Matt's voice changed when Cain described Swastika Boy and Scarman. Two of his best friends were terrified of Billy McGinty. Rita Rock was crazy to think he would ID them for her.

'Give April my best when you see her. I am sure she'll be OK,' said Matt.

'One more thing, had June Hastie harassing me.'

'What does she want?'

'Claims April was hurt in a three-in-a-bed-sex-game...'

'Was she?' asked Matt.

'Cat strangler's hawking fake news. Anything I can trade?'

'Offer her double to kill the story. If that fails, tell her you've got a movie of her fucking a fish. Most of her recent life is blacked out.'

'How do you know all this?'

'I've slept with her.'

'Video?'

'No comment.'

'Would you ...?'

'Everyone in the newsroom banged her once her star faded ... apart from you. You were in love with our Corrine. Never thought you'd fall for another until you met April. Think you love her even more.'

'Can we warn her off with a few words from tough guys? You must know people. You wrote that book about Manchester's and Salford's gangs?' asked Cain.

'You don't want to get involved in their world,' said Matt.

'Why not?'

'They are local family firms. They peddle porn, pills and powders, protection for peanuts. Most would make more working 9-5.'

'Thanks for the lecture. I'll let you know how April gets on. Second time for me. First Hannah, your goddaughter and now...'

Cain felt cheap playing the card from the bottom of the deck, but Matt deserved the sly feint of hand. 'Any information that can help me..?'

There was a slight almost indecipherable delay as Cain could sense Matt was weighing up his options. The Godfather guilt probably tipped the scales in his favour.

'I've been a crime reporter for twenty five years, Cain. Most gangsters love us glamming them up. They are dead friendly with us. Always trying to impress us with exaggerated stories. In all that time, only one man has ever really scared me. From your descriptions, I think he is the father and brother-in-law of your attackers, but never quote me.'

'His name?' asked Cain.

'Billy McGinty. Take him and his dogs very seriously,' said Matt. 'No point being in traction for six months or ending up as dog food.'

'You have a way with words.'

'McGinty is a career criminal,' said Matt. 'He stood for UKIP in a local council election once and almost won. He told the world Farage was Moses leading the white working class to the promised land. Billy's wife Violet is a former police officer turned brothel owner. She's an expert in crime detection — and avoidance.'

'What rank?' asked Cain.

'Just a constable. She's smart. Probably told him that

dogs eating the evidence avoided murder prosecutions.'

'Very funny.'

'Watch the video of a TV reporter confronting Billy and his dogs. Actually, don't.'

'Why not?'

'You won't be able to look at another dog!'

Cain liked dogs although he was wary of hounds bred to fight and kill. 'Why are we on their radar?'

'Who knows. Get off it as fast you can. Don't mess with the McGinty family, or their pets.

'This attack was out of the blue.'

'Billy is only a butcher in exceptional circumstances.'

'Such as?'

'He allegedly made his brother-in-law swallow a Samurai sword at a private party. Fed Violet's brother cold steel.'

'Just what I wanted to hear, not,' said Cain.

'You've heard the story about Jimmy Cambridge?'

'No.'

'Think Sweeney Todd.'

'The demon barber of Fleet Street who killed and served up his customers in meat pies?'

'That's the concept. Though the meat is not for humans. But food for his hunting and fighting dogs he breeds on his farm in Simister.'

'That's next door to Prestwich,' said Cain, unaware they were neighbours. Probably seen him without realising. Music femme fatale and casual racist Nico had lived in the town, but he never knew because he was too young. He must have seen her tall frame without putting two and two together. Maybe Billy helped feed her habit. Perhaps that was how he got started? 'How long has he lived there?'

'Forget where he lived. Jimmy was his best mate, but disappeared when they fell out over a deal. Not a trace of him was ever found. They were due to have a dust up in a squash court. Legend has it Billy let his dogs do the fighting. Jimmy's probably not the only notch on his bedpost. Make sure you're not the next, mate! I am being deadly serious. This is not something we can laugh off over a couple of pints.'

'I don't know what we've done to hack him off, Matt. Honestly, hand on my heart. I don't have a Scoob.'

'Does April?'

Cain could ask her, but first she had to recover from life-saving brain surgery.

Was April about to be added to McGinty's bedpost count?

He looked to the heavens and wondered if Summer's God was watching him and taking pity on the shit life threw at him.

'Fat chance,' he said out loud to himself. 'Even God was terrified of Billy McGinty and his dogs.'

Eleven.

A cautious Cain returned to the hospital with Summer and Bob after a four-hour mini break. He made sure nobody got too close on the journey to the hospital, especially people walking big dogs.

Matt Stark's anecdotal stories had spooked him. Everyone in his space was a potential McGinty gang member.

He knew he was being daft. Just because you're paranoid, doesn't mean they ain't out to get you. The saying was funny until you were the target.

Cain had never looked for trouble in his life. Much as he loved boxing, real violence and him weren't good bedfellows.

Nothing had changed in April's world. Two new nurses, veterans from foreign war zones, monitored the machines.

The trio asked for an update. A nurse said Raj would join them once he was out of theatre.

'Can she hear us?' asked Summer.

'Don't know,' said Cain. 'Can't do any harm, can it?'

'Waste of time,' said Bob. 'You're only making yourself feel good. What she needs is practical help.'

'And what's that?' asked Cain.

'I am working on it.'

'God can help.'

Dear Lord,

Your love for April is as wide as the oceans, as deep as the sea, and as tall as the heavens.

Release the full power of your spirit, let it rise like a mighty wave and come and restore my beloved April's health.

You are the water of life. You are a fresh spring.

You are healing rain to all those when April is in need.

Come, Lord, in our hour of need, show us the way....

Amen.

For a second or two, Cain envied Summer's absolute belief in the Big Man upstairs.

She moved over to him and held his arm. 'A prayer for Hannah?'

'No, thank you for asking,' said Cain. Hearing Little Miss Red Dresses' real name shocked him.

'We should always pray for loved ones.'

'Leave the man alone, Summer. He's got enough on his plate with your mum without you adding the accidental death of his daughter to the mix,' said Bob.

'What did April say about my daughter?' Cain asked Bob.

'Said your daughter was killed in a car accident in Manchester. I didn't quiz her too much, not really my business.'

'Gosh, I am sorry,' said Summer. 'Definitely should say a prayer.'

'A bit late. She's long gone.' He looked around the room

to see if she was listening to their conversation. She wasn't.

Summer was deep in prayer again. For a second, Cain thought she was taking the piss.

'Wasn't an accident. Hit and run. The driver stopped and then drove off. Not an accident in my book, you agree?' Cain asked Bob. 'Imagine if it had been Summer? I've never known anything so painful.'

'Don't,' said Summer. 'That's sick.'

'Hannah died the same day as Princess Diana.'

'Two days days after I was born,' said Summer, eyes wide at the connection.

'Everyone knows where they were when they heard about Di dying. I was lying in bed with a hangover in Prestwich. Where were you, Bob?'

'France. Wrapping up the filming of *All Down The Line*. Missed my daughter's birth.'

'Every time I see Princess Di on TV the nightmare returns,' said Cain.

'Told you this city was cursed,' said Bob.

'Perhaps we should change the subject,' said Summer. 'Hard enough dealing with mum.'

'The bloody driver got off scot free. Probably still driving pissed,' said Cain. 'People must know his name. He must have confessed. If you were him, you'd tell someone. Your best mates? Your wife?'

'I'd pray to my God. See what he would recommend,' said Summer.

'And you Bob, what would you do?' asked Cain. He could not decide if the film financier's nonchalant, disinterested demeanour was pig shit ignorance or guilt.

'I am sorry about your daughter. Sorry if I called it

an accident when it wasn't. If I recall, me and April only discussed it once three years ago. Said you wrote for a living and you'd lost your daughter. Let's talk about the Red Manifesto. Would be good to visit your restaurant, Cain,' said Bob. 'See how my investment is doing.'

'Sounds like a plan,' said Cain. What investment? He supposed it was logical for a financier to lend his former wife start up money.

He had never asked about money. She did the numbers. Asked him to provide two hundred grand for a half share of the business. He had sold his terraced house in Prestwich. Moved in with her.

Since then, she had handled finance. He did the marketing. She gave him a budget for advertising, social media and PR and he spent it as best he could. He countersigned cheques, but left the rest of the admin to her. Worked well enough for them, but they hadn't anticipated April becoming incapacitated.

They went back to silent staring-at-walls-and-mobile-screens mode. Talking about Hannah had exhausted them. Or maybe they were silently already grieving for April.

Another endless hour passed before Raj Ghandi entered the room. Apologised for keeping them waiting.

'I'll come straight to the point. We've done another electroencephalogram to determine electrical activity in April's brain,' said Raj.

'Is there?' asked Cain.

'None at the moment, but it is not sufficient to prove definitive brain death.'

'That's bad news.'

'I'll tell you straight. Two experienced doctors, myself

and another brain specialist, will carry out a series of medical tests independently. All the results have to be 'negative' before we can clinically say life has ceased.'

'Is she that close to death?' asked Summer, clutching her silver cross until her knuckles were white.

'Without brain stem activity, yes.'

'Is she already dead?' asked Cain.

'Prepare yourselves for the worst. I am really sorry.'

'When do you make the final decision?' asked Bob.

'What tests are you going to do?' asked Summer.

'Eye tests. See if she responds to a light shone a light into her eyes. We're looking for reflexes to the light.'

'She is blind in one eye. Her left,' said Cain.

'I'll check her notes. I never knew,' said Raj. 'We'll also touch April's eyelids and eyes with gauze.'

'Why?'

'See if the cornea reacts to the gauze. We'll apply cold ice water to her ears for a reaction in her eyes. We'll try pain stimulus. Different areas of the body. Try and provoke a facial reaction. All we want is one reaction to show her brain is functioning.'

'Have you done these tests already?' asked Summer.

'Yes. Some.'

'And?'

'Negative, at the moment.'

'If there is no response now, why wait?' asked Bob.

'Any reflex means April lives. Ultimately, if we disconnect her from the ventilator and the blood carbon dioxide levels increase without a breathing reflex, the brain stem is dead.'

'That's it?'

'Jesus,' said Bob.

Raj exited the room to chat to the next in line on the brain damage conveyor belt.

Cain wondered how Raj zoned out from stress? Did he turn to booze like Cain had done after Hannah's death? Or did he find comfort in religion like Summer?

'Shall we go and eat?' asked Bob. 'I could eat a horse. Do you sell horse meat at the Red Manifesto? Pass it off as prime rump? I did a film about Europeans flogging us horse meat. Cheating bloody foreigners. Only my little joke. April only used the best ingredients.'

Twelve.

The Red Manifesto was half full, or half empty, depending upon how you viewed the world through the barometer of a beer glass.

Cain ushered Bob and Summer into the restaurant. Cody came over. He introduced them.

Summer hugged her like the young do when they meet strangers.

Bob settled for an old-fashioned handshake while frog eyes bulged at her ample cleavage.

'How is she doing?' asked Cody. 'We said prayers before the shift.'

'As well as can be expected. We're all in a state of shock,' said Cain.

'Private dining is free.'

'Is Vince about?' asked Cain.

'Somewhere.'

In the private dining room, Bob picked an expensive cheeky Merlot with a whisky chaser. Summer selected Earl Grey tea.

'You and April have a really exciting brand, very vibrant. Can see why you want to roll it out,' said Bob.

'Roll it out?' asked Cain.

'Spread the gospel according to April Sands and Cain Bell. Tell the world about your Manifesto. April told me about your plans. Typically, she's invited me to add to my investment,' said Bob. 'Are you crap with money like her?'

'We're all really excited. Or we were. Everything is on hold,' said Cain, ignoring the self-made rich man's money dig. Slipped into bluff PR mode. Wasn't going to admit he didn't wear big boy trousers in the restaurant. Never knew she had a focus beyond perfecting a single site and a Michelin star. More secrets from the most beautiful woman in the world? How many more did she have?

'Manchester or further afield?' asked Summer. 'If you had one on the Wirral, I'd love to be involved.'

'Lots of different sites. Location is crucial but it has to be at the right price,' said Cain. Two can play big knobs. 'Big step investing in food retail. We target high-end consumers. They don't suffer when austerity knocks. Perhaps you're better off hedging your bets?'

'I'll simply take my money back if the expansion doesn't go ahead.' He downed the chaser, belched and asked for another.

'How can you do that?' asked Cain.

'I own the factoring company that handles your cash and does your books. The film business is fickle, like restaurants, so the business is my safety net. Everyone wants to get paid,' said Bob, a grin appeared on his face. 'Or laid.'

'I love what you've done,' said Summer. 'Why the name Red Manifesto?'

'It was our project name. Manifesto because this was the blueprint for the perfect restaurant in our eyes. The one where we would want to eat if we were given the choice. Red because we both loved Manchester United. We both supported the Labour party. And we both liked red wine. We must have tried out a thousand names before we reverted to the first.'

'I like it.'

'The brand name has obvious hints of communism too,' interrupted Bob. 'An obvious nod to Russia and China and Marxism. Crossing communism and capitalism is a very clever marketing trick, Cain. What's the one thing sets you apart from everyone else? What's your USP?'

'Well,' said Cain, red wine had loosened his tongue, but not enough to respond in kind to Bob's sly verbal kidney punches. 'Making decisions is the key to running successful restaurants. My good friend, the late great Tim Bacon, was the catalyst behind Manchester's eating out revolution. He had bought the iconic JW Johnson's before founding Living Ventures. A former Aussie child actor, with a penchant for mixing cocktails, had made his home in my city. His mantra was simple: you have got to keep making decisions. It does not matter if they are right or wrong because if you make a wrong decision and you've got the brains to decide that it is wrong you just change it for another decision and eventually you will start getting it right. That is the process of success, being prepared to make decisions and making mistakes. Muddling through was not good enough for Tim — and it isn't sufficient for me and April. Did you know Tim, Bob?'

'Australian, wasn't he? I knew everyone in the city. You don't succeed without a little help from your friends. To me

Manchester was always a stepping-stone to better things.'

A knock on the door interrupted red wine thinking. 'Daddy.' Cain saw Little Miss Red Dress.

Behind her was the giant frame of Vince Crane. 'A word, Boss, in private.'

'This is Bob Ord, April's former husband. And Summer, his daughter.'

'How you doing, Bob? Long time no see,' said Vince.

'You're looking good too, Vince. You've got bigger if that is possible. Still shagging for England?'

'Trying my hardest. You know me, Bob. Never one to miss an opportunity to bury the sword. You still making movies?'

'Films are in my blood. I'll be making them until Summer's God shouts cut.'

'You still sparking?'

'Security for Cain and April. Safer than playing with electricity.'

'You know each other?' .

'Manchester's a small village,' said Bob. 'We go back a long time. No time to get nostalgic about the past. I want to hear the names of the two men who almost killed my wife.'

Vince looked towards Cain for consent to tell the room. 'We're all family here, Vince. Have you got a name for the Swastika Boy and his mate?'

'Possibly, probably,' said Vince. He stepped into the room and shut the door behind him. 'It's very complicated and we've got some bridges to build.'

Thirteen.

Vince Crane sat himself down at the table; his enormous size dwarfed the polished woodwork.

He sighed as he struggled to form the words. Maybe his one-night stand had exhausted his tongue. Perhaps he should lend him a helping hand. Tell him the name on the tip of his tongue was Billy McGinty.

'Been interviewed twice by the police. Gave them a description of a racist youth with a Nazi tattoo and a Scar Faced older man with two smiles. A detective inspector called Rita Rock interviewed me. Wants a formal statement and identification. Any ideas?'

Cain's security head shrugged huge shoulders. The cloth of his jacked strained as his muscles expanded. 'I've been told on the QT it was an accident. A case of mistaken identity. A joke that got out of hand.'

'Really?' asked Cain. 'Who 'told' you?'

'An anonymous tip. Got to respect that request.'

'If it was a mistake, surely they can apologise? They won't mind being identified if it was an accident,' replied Cain.

'You know what dibble are like with framing people. Tell them you cannot remember what they looked like.'

'This isn't like you, Vince,' said Cain.

'Good as it gets, I am afraid. I've been asked to relay a message to you. It is up to you if you want to accept what I've told you. My advice would be to focus on April getting better,' said Vince.

'What do you think, Bob?' asked Cain.

'Listen to the man. Why would he lie to you?'

Cain knew exactly why he would lie. Like God, and everyone else in Manchester, he was scared stiff of Billy McGinty.

All the bravado bullshit was exactly that. Him and Vince were mates. Watched United together. Played arrows and backgammon.

He should respect Vince's fear. There was no point alienating Manchester's toughest doorman. 'Sure, I'll accept it as a mistake when I hear it from the horse's mouth rather than his monkey spanker.'

The second the words left his mouth, Cain regretted them. The monkey spanker phrase broke the golden rule of PR. If in doubt, say nowt.

Vince's veins in his red neck bulged ready burst. 'Give you that for free. Never diss me in public again. Before you say anything Bob, our mutual buddy asked me to say hello. Said there was no need to stay strangers.'

Vince straightened imaginary creases in his tweed jacket. Turned sharply, opened the door and left.

'What did he mean?' asked Cain, relieved Vince had ended the conversation without getting physical. Annoyed that he hadn't elaborated.

Were McGinty and Bob Ord old friends?

There was no chance for Bob to answer.

He hit the deck the moment the door closed shut. Jerked on the floor. Strides piss wet through.

Summer leaned over him. Pushed away two chairs. Whipped off her jumper. Deftly cushioned his head. The same as Nick had done for April. Checked her watch and waited. Her lips moved while she counted.

'Anything I can do?'

'No. He's not had one for ages.'

'Shall I call for an ambulance?' asked Cain.

'Be over in a couple of minutes.'

And true to her word, it was. The jerking stopped.

She placed him in the recovery position. Talked to him gently. The caustic tongued old man looked his age. 'There, there, Daddy. You'll be OK, you just had a fit. Don't worry about the smell or the wetness. I am here with Cain. Mummy's friend.'

Cain got up. Took off his black leather jacket. Offered it to Summer cover her tanned semi-nakedness.

She accepted.

He draped it over her slim shoulders. Noticed the double barbed wire tattoo wrapped around the top of her left arm. He never understood the ink attraction. At least it wasn't a swastika.

'Daddy.' Cain looked at Little Miss Red Dress perched on Bob's discarded chair. 'Why didn't you help me, like she's just helped her Dad?'

'You were already gone, Hannah, already gone. But April says the bloke who confessed to driving the car wasn't behind the wheel. Crazy isn't it?'

Fourteen.

Film legend Bob Ord was led out of the back door of the Red Manifesto.

Cain used the tradesmen's entrance to avoid the humiliation of soiled old man walking through a restaurant.

Paparazzi would have a field day cashing in on the movie mogul's humiliation. Ditto the social media mobile stalkers.

Diners didn't want to see a fellow guest had messed himself. Would spoil their dinner. Unleash a plethora of bad reviews.

Most of the restaurant's clients would have jumped to the wrong conclusion. Assumed he'd simply supped too much booze. Lost control of his bowels. 'Shall we try and clean him up?'

The incident had sobered him up.

In the taxi for the short ride home, Summer comforted her shellshocked father dressed in shiny bin liners and chef's baggy trousers. String held them up. The soiled clothes were in a black bag.

'Does it happen often?' asked Cain, as they drove down

the cobbled Castle Street. Health was the great equaliser. Wealth meant nothing if your body or mind refused to work.

'No. Hardly ever. He has medication regular as clockwork. He keeps meticulous notes. Never misses a pill,' said Summer. 'Even when he's travelling and taking care of business. He keeps it secret from most of the people he meets. They see it as mental weakness they can exploit.'

Back home, she showered and washed her father. Got him ready for bed. Cain prepared bread and fish soup from a tin for their supper.

'Can I use your washer?' asked Summer.

'Sure.'

'I should throw these trousers away except we only have overnight bags.'

'We can go shopping. There is a big Tesco in Prestwich, about twenty minutes away?'

'Cannot leave him. You cannot drive after the wine.'

Cain realised he was still holding her jumper. She was wearing his leather jacket. On her it was almost like a little black dress. 'Do you know what causes the seizures?'

'Drinks too much. Gets far too worked up about his projects. Thinks you're only as good as your last piece of work. Reputations mean nothing when you're trying to attract investors. I know him and mum are divorced, but he still shines a light for her. Never remarried. Has had more than his fair share of girlfriends, but they never last long. Never able to show his real emotions. Covers his true feelings with a joke. Are you like him?'

'Hope not,' said Cain. Bob was not his cup of tea, even if he was Hollywood-hot. He might tempt the likes of Harvey Weinstein with profitable movie investments, but the man was still probably the same chancer who started out selling snide Madchester music posters and t-shirts. 'If you need any clothes, I am sure your mother's will be a closer enough fit.'

While she checked out her mum's clothes, he placed soup bowls on the kitchen table alongside toasted baguettes with a light scattering of cheddar and parmesan with splashes of black pepper and Worcester sauce.

'This is good. Sorry about asking if you wanted to pray for Hannah earlier. Impetuous of me. Seemed a good idea when we had the Lord's attention. You know he works in mysterious ways,' she said and smiled at him just like her mother. 'My faith reassures me and I like to talk aloud to the Lord with prayer. Done it all my life.'

'If it helps...,' said Cain.

'We could say a joint prayer for April and Hannah now if you wanted?'

'No, it's fine. Suppose religion is another form of counselling,' said Cain. 'Must have been difficult living a peripatetic lifestyle with your parents constantly on the move.'

'They banished me to boarding school from an early age. Long distance parenting was standard. The price of international heroes running around saving the planet while ignoring their own flesh and blood, not that I am bitter,' smiled Summer. 'I've only got to know her in the last three years or so since she stayed in the same place for a prolonged period of time. Now I am going to lose her because of a silly case of mistaken identity and silly japes getting out of hand.'

'You won't,' said Cain. He held her close to him as reassuringly as he could, already sick of the mistaken identify narrative. 'She saved my life in a hotel room in Japan and we'll do what we can to save hers.'

'How did she save your life?'

'It's a long, short story that involves sushi, sake and a post-coital kiss of life. Stop me if I get too graphic.'

Fifteen.

Loud snoring from the second guest room made it tough to think.

How could Cain reveal how April saved his life without sounding salacious?

He looked out of the large window at the light show below.

Silent rain pounded superior treble glazing.

Anyone sleeping rough tonight would get drenched. Nick was out there, kipping on cold concrete.

He walked over to the drinks cabinet. Opened it. 'Do you want one?' he asked Summer, unsure how he should start the story about April rescuing him.

'Teetotal. Through choice. My faith doesn't forbid drink, but it feels right. Like always telling the truth because the Lord is always with me.'

If the Lord was watching him, he would be disgusted he had allowed Nick Forti to sleep rough. A real man would go and get him. Help him sort out his problems. Not look the other way after he had selflessly put his own life on the line.

He sat down again, opposite the exhausted daughter of the most beautiful woman in the world and decided to busk.

'Hannah was my daughter, taken from us on the day Princess Diane was killed in Paris, France. My daughter was the perfect ten. We were walking to the off-licence, minding our own business as you do. I was talking to her mum on the phone. She had been running a big event in Manchester for a legal firm. I was checking what wine she wanted for supper. We were going to cross the road at a pelican crossing. I heard the engine noise and the thud. Hannah was thrown up in the air. She travelled thirty two feet before she landed on her head. They told me her neck snapped upon impact and killed her outright. She wouldn't have suffered or known anything about it.'

'I am so sorry.' Summer had taken a small hanky from her jeans pockets. Wiped her eyes and her nose.

'After the impact I thought the car would stop. The driver would realise what he had done. Would get out the car. He appeared to reduce his speed. Then accelerated away. At the inquest, the police said he was doing between forty and fifty when he hit Hannah.'

'How long did he get?'

'Police never caught him. Nobody wanted the reward money the police offered. Just a huge wall of silence, even though it happened on a busy Saturday night in a busy suburban town,' said Cain.

'Must have been unbearable?'

'Numbness first. Just like now with your mum. That's not sunk in and it didn't sink with my own daughter. Me and her mum never talked about the hit and run. Never. Just drifted apart completely within six months and she moved to Australia, remarried and never came back. Once my wife Corrine had gone, I started a long-term relationship with hedonism. I never discussed Hannah with anyone. When people asked if I had kids, I'd lie. Say I fired blanks. Easier than explaining...'

'Didn't you have grief counselling?'

'No. You're right. I am like your father. In Manchester men frown upon bleeding hearts. I was back ambulance chasing within a week. I was good reporting grief because I never got emotionally involved, even with my own daughter's murder.'

'That's horrible. Shall we pray?'

'Let me finish. Please,' said Cain. He didn't want to stop in case he lost his thread.

She nodded at him and wiped her eyes again.

'Your mother and me bumped into each other in Japan. We'd lived all those years in Manchester, but never met. Yet here we were six thousand miles from home. I was doing PR for Global Manchester at an international exhibition. She was working as a development chef for a big USA corporate. We met at Sukiyabashi Jiro where they zip you through the tasting menu of about 20 small courses. I was pissed. Told her I fancied the bits off her and always had done all my life even though it was the first time I'd ever seen her. After we'd eaten, we talked and danced and talked and drank and talked. It was such fun and she was easy company and I wanted her to join my imperfect girl club. Are you OK me talking about this?'

'Sure.' She left the words unsaid, like her mother would have done if she was sat there in her place. April knew how to use space in conversations. Knew when to speak and when to let the silence do the talking. He was the opposite.

'We ended up in her hotel room and did what adults do. Afterwards, I was having a cigarette on the balcony and just started talking about Hannah, like I was talking to you a minute ago. She got it straight away, understood me and told me there was nothing wrong in feeling numb. There was nothing wrong in wanting to see her. I told your mum I see Hannah sometimes. I said I know she's not there. I know she is dead. And I know it's just my imagination playing with me. But I like seeing her in the red dress and red coat she wore on that night. Your mum said she would picture her too so we could share the experience. I described her and she said she could see her in her mind. Said she was a beautiful child.'

'How beautiful.'

'After the balcony confession we went back to bed. I'd never felt like this before with a woman, until my chest exploded. Next thing I know, I am in hospital after heart surgery and guess who is waiting for me to wake up?'

'My mum?'

'Yes.'

'How romantic.'

'She stayed with me. Quit her job. Moved to Manchester. We opened the Red Manifesto six months later. I'd never dreamed I would have the gonads to do such a thing. Or that it would work, and we would be named restaurant of the year. And she agreed to marry me. You know, less than 48 hours ago, I thought nothing could ruin my second chance at happiness. And look at me now? Broken.'

'Shall we pray?'

'No, I need some fresh air. Thanks for listening,' said

Cain, without adding he'd only told her half the real story.

The chest pains and breathlessness had been with him for several weeks. There were pains in his shoulders and he felt sick much of the time … he knew he was ill but didn't care.

He had no reason to live until April bounced into his life.

He stood up went to get his coat from the cupboard near the front door. Fiddled with his coat while he heard her pray.

Lord, visit me and Cain today and give us faith to believe that his child Hannah who served you faithfully for such a short time is in your presence, and he will see and love her again. Remove anger and bitterness from his heart and help him accept the demise of our Hannah brings her closer to you. Forgive the man who drove the car and hope he has found the light too. Nullify Cain's pain and fill our hearts with your shining light. Help us to walk in love and fill us with joy everlasting. Lord, turn my mourning into dancing by offering us eternal hope. Help me mum too so she and Cain can love each other under your watchful eye. Let them be united as one. Protect them from evil at all times. Amen.

He wasn't religious. Didn't have a religious bone in his body. Never believed in an afterlife or a resurrection.

But he had believed one hundred per cent in karma until April's revelation about Ted Blake made him doubt natural justice.

Mistaken identity boiled his piss.

Why would a man about to die lie? And why would the a detective in Manchester corrupt himself? If he had?

Perhaps April was lying or had been told lies and was repeating them to him. He needed to get outside and walk the stress out of his legs.

Sixteen.

Outside, the hard rain and bitter wind hit him hard. How could you sleep outside in this? Thousands did.

Cain pulled his coat's collar tight around his neck. Rammed his woollen hat hard on his head and gritted his teeth.

His mission was simple.

Find Nick and offer him sanctuary from the wind and the rain. he knew where he had been dossing down on the night of the attack, and assumed he would still be there.

Head down, he crossed Deansgate at the Liverpool Road junction. Speed walked under Bridge 100 to a small tented encampment.

Carefully, he approached. 'Nick? Are you in there? It's me, Cain Bell. We met last night.'

'I am over here.'

'Where?'

'In the bushes. Having a dump. Really bad Ruby Murray.' The voice was a whisper. 'How's April doing?'

'Touch and go. They said you saved her life.'

'Did they give you odds?'

'They are not sure if she is…brain dead.'

'Shit. When will they know?'

'When the drugs wear off.'

'Thought you could keep warm and dry in the apartment?'

'You not wanting to bum me?'

'You what?'

'Paper for my bum. I know it's windy. In the tent. Left hand side by the gas stove.'

Cain peered into the undergrowth. The noise of the wind and whispered urgency caused uncertainty. Delayed his movement towards the tent.

Would a homeless man have loo paper? Gas stoves in tents was more Glastonbury than Cardboard City.

The gas fireball pushed him backwards. He could not defy the physics.

Let himself fall. Let his weight take him under the water. Closed his mouth to avoid swallowing dirty water. Let his momentum stop before he floated to the surface. Exhaled and breathed in the precious oxygen.

He looked for ladders out of the canal on the left-hand side. There were none.

The voice in the bushes had known about April. Cain had assumed it was Nick. He should have been more on his guard. Another case of mistaken identity? Like fuck.

'I'll give you a hand.' A dark thick set figure in a hood stood where he had fallen in. 'Come on mate. Swim over here.'

'Was anyone in the tent?' asked Cain.

'Get out of the water, then we'll look.'

Cain swam towards the bank. Held out a hand and was

pulled from the water with ease. Tall as he was, his helper had no problem shifting his weight.

'There you go, mate. Not sure what happened with that gas cooker exploding like that. Pure accident. You were dead lucky. Pisspots like Nick are a danger to themselves and everyone around them.'

The hooded figure kicked the gas cylinder out of the tent. The fire had been extinguished by the heavy rain.

'Was Nick ..?'

Before he could move, Cain was pushed gently from behind. There was at least two of them. He was prodded towards the wrecked tent.

He didn't resist. Had to play this out as best he could. If they wanted to hurt him, they would have done it by now. 'What's going on? Where's the bloke who lived here?'

'Moved to a new pitch,' said Swastika Boy from behind. He recognised the voice immediately. The lazy insolent speech copied from Liam Gallagher, Shaun Ryder and daft old Bez. 'Who are you?'

'We're your new best friends come to give you some very sensible advice.' Cain felt cold steel on his face. 'Last night was a case of mistaken identity. You don't talk to the police. And you don't identify anybody unless it is n*****s, pakies or jew boys. Understand?'

'Yes.' Cain nodded. Of course, he did. Knives made arguments very one-sided.

'Dibble may tell you they can protect you, but they can't and they won't. Your man Vince is our gimp. How is your bride doing anyway?'

'Hospital.'

'Make sure you don't join her.'

Cold steel on his cheek was gone. Cain wanted to throw up, except the man who had pulled him out of the water was still stood in front of him, face half hidden by his hoodie. 'What's this all about? I don't know any of you. Never asked for trouble. Never looked for it. You're not Billy McGinty, are you?'

The hooded figure laughed. 'I am a saint compared to Billy.'

He moved forwards and gently nodded his head. Caught the bridge of Cain's nose with a glancing blow that surprised more than it hurt.

"Fuck."

His voice hissed like a rattlesnake. 'That butt was for show for Nobby. Didn't hurt you too bad so don't start crying. Whatever state April is in, isn't down to us. Forget the filth. Forget telling your mates. You tell that to my sister when she asks. Now off you fuck and get yourself dry. You'll catch your death of cold in this bloody rain.'

Seventeen.

Exhausted, Cain stepped into the walk-in shower fully dressed.

He power-showered away the stench of the canal water from his clothes and stripped.

Chucked them out of the shower and stood under the hot stream.

Relived the unambiguous words hissed into his ears. The blade against his cheek.

How did ordinary, average men counteract violent intimidation? They didn't. They froze or they ran. There was no retaliation unless you knew how to hurt them more than they could hurt you.

He wiped the shower's mirrored wall to give himself a quick MOT.

His nose was tender. Torso bruised from tumbling down. Hands grazed from scratching at brick walls. The damage inside his head was less obvious.

The thugs had targeted her on purpose although only she could tell him and she wasn't going to be doing that in a hurry, if ever. She'd told him she could no longer live a lie with him, whatever that meant. He didn't know, but the McGinty clan might.

April had said she knew who drove the car night and it wasn't Ted Blake. Who would April have confided in?

There was one obvious choice a trained journalist should have spotted. They had argued the night he had proposed. Question was, did psychiatrist Rachel Roberts take calls at 4am in the morning?

He didn't test her. Only people who were bonkers or off their tits called at that time of the morning.

After his shower, he went online and searched for Rachel Roberts in April's email to see if money was owed. Settling a debt was an easy 'in' and an obvious reason to call.

There was.

Cain waited until 7am. Sent Rachel an email saying he had April's ton fifty in cash, and he could bring it round as she lived in St Mary's Parsonage close to Kendals.

He was heading in that direction on the way to the hospital.

She responded within 10 minutes. Said she worked out at the fitness gym in Quay Street and they could chat in an hour's time.

Rachel Roberts was waiting for him when he arrived. She was dressed in vivid purple and pink lycra. Her face glistened with beads of sweat and she sniffed constantly.

'Thanks for seeing me at such short notice,' said Cain. 'A cold?'

'Hay fever. Late Autumn pollen.'

'Must be a pain.'

'Drank a little too much last night. A natural reaction

when a friend is hurt. How is she doing? How are you doing?'

'She might be brain dead. A definitive diagnosis can only be made once the sedation drugs have left her body.'

Rachel's eyes spontaneously overflowed. Tears raced down her razor-sharp cheek bones. Messed up her mascara leaving black tracks in their wake. 'She's constantly been in my thoughts and prayers. The moment I heard. You too.'

'Who told you?'

'Can't remember. Rumours spread through this town in the blink of an eye.'

'What did you and April talk about?' asked Cain. 'Anything to change my opinion of her?'

'I cannot say without her permission.'

'But she is in no state to agree. Soon she might be dead.'

'Client confidentiality stays with her. If I told you, my reputation would be finished. Nobody would trust me. My Hippocratic oath is not taken lightly.'

Cain nodded and decided to change the subject. He'd leave his key question until the end of the interview, an old journalistic trick. 'How do I cope if she dies?'

'Recovery starts with this conversation.'

'How do you mean?' asked Cain, expecting a pitch to win his business.

'Bereaved people try to go back to being normal far too soon. They forget to give themselves time to grieve and mourn.'

'What's going to happen to me if she dies?'

'You're going to be traumatised for a couple of weeks before the actual grief sets in so you don't need to try to articulate how you feel or even apologise to me or anyone else. But I am here to tell you it will be OK and to reassure you, you'll come out of this, no matter how bad you feel right now. What I am trying to say, is you need to wait at least a year, or possibly longer before you access therapy that will help you mourn rather than grieve.'

'Thank you.' He smiled at her. If he was a gambling man, he had just lost his bet. She wasn't pitching for work. She was telling him to be patient and let time control the healing process. 'How do I know that will work?'

'Time healed me when my husband drowned on holiday in St Lucia. I was on a private beach, waving at him while he swam and waved back. I never blamed the hotel or the travel agent for not warning us about the water. We should have known except we were too much in lust to find out. Now, two and a half decades on, I don't remember his ordinary everydayness. Nor his smell. I can't really remember the sound of his voice and I refuse to watch our wedding video or look at old photographs. Fortunately, he died before social media became an obsession. I do occasionally dream about him screwing me. His big hard cock inside me when he drilled me all night long. I am a Freudian thinker – not boys shagging their mums, but I do believe dreams reflect our true wishes. Part of me wants him back, although that will never happen. Maybe in my next life after the resurrection I'll be the hard cock with the power to penetrate. I am also a good Catholic girl too. Am I being too blunt? Men can be studs and talk about shagging but women…we're slags, sluts and whores.'

'Not at all. What were you arguing about in the restaurant on the night she was attacked?'

'My choice of shag … too close to home.'

'How close?'

'That's private.'

He nodded. Reached into the inside pocket of his black leather jacket. Pulled out seven twenties and one ten. Passed the money to her. S

he went to take the cash. He placed his left hand on top of hers. Moved closer so he could look into her reddish bluey green eyes. 'How much for you to tell me about your sessions with April?'

'Nothing. She's still alive. And she's still my client.'

'And if she dies?'

'She's in my thoughts and prayers. You too,' said Rachel.

'Think about it,' said Cain.

The conversation hadn't ended like he had anticipated, but he had planted seeds.

Eighteen.

Cain felt semi-chuffed as he left the gym and dodged millennial serfs rushing to keep fit before a day's graft.

Planting seeds was the basis for all good PR. Rachel Roberts' eyes, runny nose and anxious demeanour implied she might need cash to feed a habit.

He could hook her if the price was right.

Back at the apartment Summer, unchanged from the previous day, cooked and hummed *Abide With Me* under her breath.

Bob, dressed in one of April's dressing gowns, whistled his own version of the tune, free from any epileptic fit hangover from the previous night.

'After breakfast I need to shop and buy some underwear and togs for Pops,' Summer said. 'Then we can go to the hospital together. I checked when you were out and there is no change.'

When Summer left to go shopping, Bob Ord strolled into living room, barely able to contain his excitement. He held an iPad in his hand.

'I'll not fanny about. My insurance people have agreed to fund a private clinic in California.'

'Subject to medical approval from Raj?'

'Soon as she can travel, my health insurers will get her in front of the very best brain specialists in the entire universe.'

'What if she stays in a coma or is brain dead?'

'We wait until the science improves. Freeze her.'

'Hold on, Bob, you're going too fast.'

'I'll speak slower. This is the Emily Frances Head Injury Clinic in southern California; the best medical care centre in the world for serious head injuries. I have reserved a place for April with stunning beach views overlooking the Pacific Ocean less than an hour ago. The room is ready and waiting for her whenever we fly her over. Look ...'

'All within 24 hours ..?'

'There is more. A very good film producer friend of mine needs a new head of corporate PR. I think you'd be an ideal replacement given your track record as a journalist and as a public relations officer. He agrees. Hal's package would double or even treble what you're currently earning.'

'Why?'

'April can make a full recovery at the Emily Frances Head Injury Clinic.'

'Why do all this for me?'

'Not for you.'

'For my former wife and my daughter. Summer will have lots of opportunities in California. There are lots of contacts in Hollywood. That's why she does her God Squad act. All about perception. Like you and your Mr Chilled act. Both of you could build your careers and help return April to full health. Stay at our house as long as you don't start shagging my daughter. She's not part of the deal. My joke. I don't care if you do. Just an exchange of fluids. I would ... if she wasn't my flesh and blood. Another joke. Let me show you the house.'

Bob flicked through another slide show. Revealed an equally stunning expensive coastal residence.

'Impressive,' said Cain, unsure if he was really impressed or just being polite.

'Our home has massive oceanfront decks with endless spectacular views where you can enjoy warm California sun, not bloody freezing Manchester despair. And it is all yours and Summer's. We agreed? I'll tell Raj when we meet up in a bit?'

'I don't know what to think,' said Cain. This was out of the blue. Money could do this within 24 hours. The police had offered a ten-grand reward for news about Hannah and Bob could spaff the same on a non-returnable deposit on a bed that might stay empty.

'Thank me later.'

'What did Summer say?'

'Loves the idea. Secretly, she likes you as you too, you know what I mean?'

Cain did and he didn't. He smiled and assumed Bob's salacious head was messed up by his meds. 'What about my life here? My business. My apartment. My friends. My social life. Manchester is my home.'

'Manchester is a cursed cesspit full of losers. This city of shit contaminates everyone who comes into contact with it. You can have a better life in LA with me championing you. You can see it, can't you?'

Cain didn't know what to think. Bob's proposition

crackpot crazy yet totally sensible. Mental to be talking about the future when April's fate hung in the balance. 'I don't know what to say. Generous beyond belief.'

'You'll be free.'

'That easy?'

Bob was right. Forget all about the McGinty family. Matt Stark had hit the nail very hard on the head.

Their reach didn't extend five thousand miles across the Atlantic Ocean and the width of America. Their infamy was confined to the M60's inner circle. Beyond their reputations meant nothing.

If Cain left England, he would never look over his shoulder again. New job. New life. New chances for him and April. Little Miss Red Dress could come too.

'You and Summer can be there tomorrow. I'll hold the fort in England until they transfer April. We have a deal?'

'What about Red Manifesto?'

'We'll run it together until April is back on her feet. I'll find you a general manager after you've flown out. I've got connections in this city, even of it is cursed. I know a lot of good people, the best people.'

Nineteen.

His head was spinning. Bob was offering him a way out.

All he had to do was say yes. Collect the airline tickets and fly out of the country never to return.

If anybody wanted to whinge, he'd be well out of earshot. It was that easy.

The mobile rang. He answered. It was Rita Rock. There was no reference to their previous conversation.

Did he want to make a formal ID statement? She said they would be releasing details of the attack as part of their standard daily police crime briefings this morning. As a former reporter, he knew the score.

She said the sooner he spoke formally to the police, the better. What time could he come in?

He told her he would call from the hospital after he had an update on April's condition.

Rita hid her obvious disappointment and said she would be available when he was free. She said she worked flexible shifts. This was so important that she was free any hour of the day or night.

He was stalling and playing for time. They both knew it. Bob's offer could not have come at a better time.

Once the police press release landed, it was open season. The relative privacy of the last 36 hours would be washed away when the story went live.

A possible celebrity murder story had clickbait orgy potential. The feelings of those involved were secondary to clicks, reads, likes, shares and the illiterate unintelligible opinions of wanky keyboard warriors.

He reckoned the chick-chef-in-a-coma would go viral.

If June Hastie added her three-in-a-bed sex romps it would go double viral. She'd been quiet.

He had time for a bit of pre-emptive PR action to lessen the shitstorm that was about to break.

He put an auto-responder on the mobile for texts. Changed the voicemail message on the phone. Explained that although April was in hospital, she was expected to be out within a week.

Updates would be posted on the Red Manifesto website and social media platforms.

He placed holding messages online. He emailed the Red Manifesto senior management team. Any queries had to be passed to the general manager.

He called Cody. Briefed her about press enquiries. Business as usual. They expected April to make a full recovery.

The mobile rang. Talk of the devil. 'Hello Cain, your story is live on the newswire,' said June Hastie. 'Have you got a comment about April's injuries being caused by sex games with homeless men?' She was back on the hunt for red top salacious crap. 'Just checked your website and it says she's not seriously injured and you expect her home soon.'

'I am about to go and see her. Do you fancy lunch at the Unicorn near Afflecks Palace? I am buying.'

She hesitated. Cain knew she was weighing up her options. Free booze would not interfere with the syndication of her salacious scoop. If nobody else had access to her source, she controlled the clock. 'See you about two. You'd better give me something good.'

The phone rang again. He thought it was her again. 'What do you want, June? I said we'd meet at 2pm.'

'It's me. Vince. Who is June?' Cain quickly explained. He didn't want to waste time chatting to Vince. Not when he had decisions to make. Could he really just fly away from Manchester? 'Do you want me to have a word with her?'

'No,' said Cain.

'We need to negotiate a truce as soon as possible.'

'Who with?'

'Face-to-face only, mate.'

'I am going to the hospital to see April.'

'I'll see you there,' said Vince.

The call ended as abruptly as it started.

Before he could collect his thoughts, Summer breezed in. Laden with shopping bags from Selfridges and Harvey Nichols. Dumped them in the middle of the living room. Asked her father if he had discussed their plan with Cain.

'Yes,' said Bob.

'And you agreed?' she asked Cain.

'He never said no,' replied Bob.

'You know it makes sense, Cain. It is the cleverest plan ever devised by Pops.'

She handed two of the bags to her father. 'Underpants, trousers and shirts. Now what dress shall I wear to see Mum?'

She whipped off her jumper and jeans and performed her very own private fashion show, modelling several modest midi dresses, one of which was the obligatory black number, the others more colourful and flowery.

Perhaps she had modelled professionally and stripping naked behind the catwalk was part of the job description.

Her father joined in and started trying on his new gear, stripping and dressing in the living room although he wore underwear. 'Who is the best model, Cain? You judge?' asked Bob, as he struck a pose and then another.

Summer emulated her father as they tried to out-camp each other. 'Does age trump young beautiful flesh?'

'I didn't buy you anything because I wasn't sure of your sizes. But we'll get you a completely new wardrobe in California. We'll see mum and then start packing. You are coming with me? Will be a right laugh and mum will make a miracle recovery with God's help.'

Cain wanted to ask if their American God was smarter than the Brit version, but decided to keep it zipped.

Why shatter their positivity with a dose of northern reality if they were going to pick up the tab?

Did he fancy being a kept man?

He wasn't sure there were any alternatives.

Twenty.

Vince Crane waited outside the front entrance of the North Manchester General Hospital.

He was a picture of health and wealth compared to dozens of sneaky coffin-dodging patients who sucked on life-affirming smokes against doctor's orders.

Cain spotted him straight away. Stood slightly apart from the unfortunates attached to wheelchairs, oxygen masks and mobile drips on metal sticks.

He thought that in a parallel universe Vince could have been a crooner, a country singer or a movie star with a banjo on his knee. No wonder a certain type of woman was attracted to his macho overkill.

Away from work, Vince had ditched the country squire look and was clad in bomber jacket, black jeans, black tee and quick apologies.

'Sorry about the harsh words last time we spoke. We were all bit tense, one thing and another. I've got a name,' said Vince.

'So have I,' replied Cain.

'This conversation is between you and me. Agreed?'

'Why?'

'Never took place. Yes or no?'

'OK. But why is it important?'

'I'll tell you a very long story quickly. I was a bit of a lad back home in Ireland when I was a youngster, barely old enough to shave. I was a big time Champagne Charlie, helping everyone else have a good time too. Anyway, I upset some boys on the local army council and they wanted to make an example. Fortunately, I had a few friends who stood up for me. They exiled me permanently rather than shoot off my kneecaps. You cannot believe how grateful I was to get on the ferry to Liverpool without being on permanent crutches or worse, disappeared in an unmarked hole in the middle of nowhere. Never been back home, in twenty-five years. My folks and friends come to me rather than risk me getting hurt, you know what I mean, Cain?'

'Not really.'

'What I am trying to say is we have a similar situation here.'

'We're in exile?'

'No, but somehow we've annoyed similar people to the local army council. People who never go away. Who never forget, who never forgive. And who can always reach you, no matter how hard you try to hide.'

'Sorry, Vince, but I am being dead thick here,' said Cain. 'Call a spade a spade.'

'Somebody connected to your attacker reached out to me. Said I didn't need to know who carried out the attack. Nor did you. They were very sorry April was hurt and all that, but it is what it was and now we both had to forget about it. No police. No social media bullshit. No selling our stories to the newspapers. Or appearing on TV crying our eyes out offering cash rewards.'

'Just like that?'

'Yes.'

'Thankfully, it is not your problem,' said Cain.

'That's where you are wrong.'

'How come?'

'I was told I am responsible for you,' said Vince.

'No names?' asked Cain, seeing if Vince would finger the McGinty family without being prompted.

'Telling you as a friend, a good friend. One you need to listen to very carefully.'

'Why me? Why us? Me and April?'

'Damned if I know.'

'I need to go and see April.'

'You'll take my advice?' asked Vince.

'Sure,' said Cain. 'Catch you later. Thanks for the chat. I never identified Ryan McGinty or Liam Devlin.'

He watched Vince's face for the expected look of surprise. There was none. Nor was there the usual happy-go-lucky grin.

'That's a smart move, Cain. You're not as dumb as you look.'

'Are the McGintys that scary that they even terrify you, Vince?'

Again, there was no reaction from Vince. Just a look of absolute resignation.

'You don't want to go to war with Billy McGinty. You'll never win. Never, in a million years.'

'What's your answer? Are you scared of them? Nothing

to be ashamed of — they terrify me too if I am being honest about it.'

'I am scared of no-one, but I also want to stay alive and not be fed to the dogs.'

'What do mean?'

'Ask your friend Matt Stark about Jimmy Cambridge. If you want to talk to them, I can arrange it, but if you cross them, they will hurt you. And probably me as well.'

'They've already hurt me all they can.'

'Think of the worst possible pain you could ever have and then double it again and again. Mark my words they don't do half measures when they want something. Nothing or nobody gets in their way.'

Twenty-One.

Inside the hospital's ICU nothing had changed from his last visit.

April was lying in bed as if she was dozing on a lazy Sunday morning with the newspapers and the radio.

Were the nurses around her less intense, slightly more relaxed?

Had the critical care been stepped down?

Did they know about the plans to send her to the USA?

Summer was holding her mother's hand, whispering about a new life in California as if it was a done deal.

'Have you told anyone else about your plans, apart from God?' asked Cain.

'Pops and the insurance company are handling the paperwork. God says it is a great idea.'

Cain noticed Summer kept nipping at the fleshy part of April's hand. 'Why are you doing that?'

'Waiting for the miracle God is sending our way,' whispered Summer. 'I can trust you one hundred percent Cain. We both want the same thing, don't we?'

'Sure.'

'Pops thinks the doctors want to turn the machines off before we're ready. They want to harvest her organs because they'll get paid for the transplant operations. If that happens, we are ready. Miracles happen, despite what the science says. I refuse to accept she is brain-dead based on a silly scan. Jesus rose from the dead at Easter without any fancy scans and so will my mum. I believe God will intervene if we reach out to him. He is busy, but he will help when he has the time. Are you going to help me, Cain Bell?' she asked, her voice barely audible.

'How?'

'We tell them she responds to our touch.'

'We lie? I thought God demanded truth?'

'Yes, but he is OK if it is for the greater good. Will be our secret. But we never, ever tell anyone. Not even mum when she recovers and is back living on happy hill.'

'How are we going to fool experienced doctors? They'll know.'

'So what if they do? Once she is on that plane, they can whistle until the cows come home.' Cain nodded gently. Looked at April asleep, blissfully unaware of her plight. If she had been, would she have been proud of her daughter? 'We need to talk this through in private,' she said.

'When?'

'Sooner, rather than later. But not here.'

'She cannot hear us,' said Cain. He nodded slightly towards April.

'The nurses can. They must get it all the time,' said Summer, her voice below even a whisper.

They walked to the Costa in the labyrinth of corridors

that snaked around the sprawling North Manchester General Hospital site.

Took them five minutes and three false turns. He spotted Nick Forti in the far corner. Hospital visitors and patients were repulsed by homeless alcoholics wherever they saw them. 'Can you get me a flat white. I need to have a private word with a friend over there.' Cain went across. 'Anyone sat here? How are you doing?'

Nick Forti looked up. Fresh cuts and bruises, black eyes and sutures. 'You should see the other fella, or should I say fellas,' he said. 'Sit down. You're hurting my neck.'

Cain did as he was told. Glanced over to Summer, who was playing with her mobile. 'Never knew you resurrected your boxing career. I was looking for you last night. What happened?'

'Jumped from behind. I curled up into a ball and took the kicking.'

'Because of me and April?'

'I was lucky they didn't set me on fire.'

'They burned your tent. I think the boy who put April in a coma threatened me.'

'Ryan McGinty?'

'Did you tell the police?'

Nick Forti shook his head. Grimaced through the pain on his face. 'Why ignore my first and final warning?'

'From…?'

'Billy. I thought I recognised his nipper by the canal, but I wasn't sure.'

'You know the people involved? The McGintys?'

'Everyone knows them in my social circles.'

'Did Ryan do this to you?'

'Him, Two Smiles and a couple of others. Said Billy liked me otherwise I'd be sucking cold soup through a plastic straw. Said I shouldn't have interfered. Said the whole episode was an accident best forgotten.'

'I am sorry,' said Cain. Nick didn't need the aggro. Had enough problems without being used as a human football.

'Not your fault.'

'I'll give you money for a holiday. How much?' asked Cain. He could call it a discretionary marketing spend. Nobody would mind. April wasn't checking any day soon.

'Thanks but I don't have a passport.'

'Must be able to do something for you.'

'Steer clear of Billy McGinty,' said Nick.

'Do you know him, personally?'

'Our paths have crossed when I boxed. He wanted me to do a Sonny a couple of times?'

'A Sonny?'

'Fall over to order like Sonny Liston. He was beaten twice by Ali, although he was the favourite both times. Second time he was felled by a phantom punch. Billy said it was for the betting money. Said he ended with a spike in his arm because nobody likes to hear blacks speaking out of turn. We all got to know our place. He has this way with him, does Bill. Like he asked me to take an early tumble, without actually saying the words. All implied. He's smart, as well as brutal.'

'Did you dive?' asked Cain.

'Nobody cares. We've all moved on.'

'Could explain the drink and the sleeping around?

'Are you my shrink now?' Nick picked up his coffee. Drank gingerly. Tried, unsuccessfully, to disguise his pain.

'Only trying to help,' said Cain.

'The people who did Universal Credit said the same thing when they wanted me to clean bogs in this shithole hospital for a minimum bloody wage. I am a trained butcher. I fought for two world titles. I made a lot of people a lot of money, but they all look the other way, only Billy … he offered me work guarding his massage parlours. Me and Sonny both had punching power and an eye for milky white skirt. I would have owed them more than they paid me.'

'You're his friend?'

'Nobody's Billy's friend.'

'First name terms, at least,' said Cain, spotted the contradiction. Nick had been beaten up on the orders of his 'friend'.

'Your daughter wants you,' said Nick. He looked in the direction of Summer. 'You'd be a good father. Give my ears a breather from your incessant chatting.'

'My only daughter died in a hit and run accident,' said Cain. He reached into his back pocket. Counted two hundred. Passed the notes to Nick.

'I am very sorry,' said Nick. 'I didn't know.' He pushed the money back towards Cain.

'That is an advance on your wages. I am hiring you at the Red Manifesto as my eyes and ears. I might be going away for a holiday and I need someone I can trust to look after things for me,' said Cain.

'I can't accept charity.'

'You'd be helping me out a lot.'

'Where are you going?'

'The USA.'

'Where?'

'California. April's rehab,' said Cain, testing the water to see if his trip sounded sane. 'They have booked her a place in a specialist brain unit. You can help me out again. I can trust you. One of the few people who ain't out to rip me off. Bunk down at mine until we find you some digs. Think about it. I'll finish my coffee.'

Cain stood up. Walked over to Summer. Deliberately sat down with his back to Nick. Took the cup nearest him. Sipped it slowly. 'Tell me if he picks up the money on the table.'

'Who is he?' asked Summer.

'The man who saved me and your mum.'

'I should thank him.'

'You can do that at home. He's coming to stay with us and I've given him a job,' said Cain.

He knew Nick was a proud man who would rather eat worms than accept a handout from a snowflake. But everybody needed friends in their hour of need.

'We say mum's left eyelid flutters with a busy nurse an immediate witness. When they tell the doctors it becomes their story not ours. We play the whole scene really low key,' said Summer. 'The less involved we are, the better.'

'You've thought this through.'

'Deception is not rocket science, just common sense.'

'When do we do this?'

'We need a codeword. When I say 'beach' follow my lead.'

'Manchester has everything you want in life, apart from a beach, that sort of thing?' asked Cain.

'Exactly, we're on the same song sheet.'

'He's leaving,' said Summer.

'Who?'

'Your friend. You asked me to tell you…'

Cain turned as Nick Forti picked up the money from the table.

He carried his coffee container to the rubbish tray. Placed it in the bin.

Cain glanced towards the table where the boxer had sat. Little Miss Red Dress was there by herself, sulking. She refused point blank to acknowledge him. Not even a quick wave or a semi-smile. She had ignored him for twenty-four hours. Her disdain was obvious for everyone to see.

Nick limped over to Cain and Summer. 'We've got a deal,' said Nick. 'I did what McGinty ordered and regretted it every day since. Was not the same man after I took a bribe. Got me a house I don't live in. Some might say I owe him one like you do, although I am big on forgiveness.'

Forgiving the McGinty family wasn't on Cain's songsheet. Same forgiveness hadn't been on the agenda with Ted Blake.

Question was, how did you square off to Manchester's nastiest gangster and win?

Bottom line was you didn't and if you had any sense you ran. Nobody would think any less of him apart from Little Miss Red Dress who only existed in his head.

She'd do whatever he told her to do.

Apart from paying attention to a driver who was not paying attention himself. Bloody Ted Blake had sounded so convincing.

Described the little red dress Hannah was wearing and where she had landed.

Whoever had primed Ted must have been there themselves.

Twenty-Two.

She had gone. The bed was empty. Her nursing staff were occupied with other patients.

An extended coffee break had caught them napping. Bob was sat there, oblivious, doing a crossword on a folded broadsheet.

'Where is she?' Summer asked the nearest nurse in a loud whisper.

'Gone for a scan,' she replied. 'You cannot have four visitors at the same time.'

'It's OK, Sue,' said Raj. He appeared from behind a curtain, his reassuring smile muted. 'What's going on? Men in suits want to fly April to California.'

'Yes,' said Bob. 'Is there a problem with that?'

'No, but …'

'Good.'

'We're still responsible for her,' said Raj. He made no attempt to hide his anger. 'There are still drugs in April's body that might potentially alter the results of the scan. Lack of brain activity could be down to them.'

'When can we have her?' asked Bob.

'Tomorrow at the earliest,' said Raj.

Cain could see him give up the fight. Beaten in the same way Nick Forti must have felt after he took the dirty money to throw a fight.

He had just done the same. Let her former husband and daughter dictate April's future. Not that he could blame Raj. Cain knew nobody won against big money and corporate insurance lawyers.

'I'll need all the paperwork in place before I can release her.'

'I need some space,' said Cain. It was all too much to see the resignation in Raj's eyes after all he had done to save her life.

He should have said something to console him, but any words would have been tokenism.

Tackling June's threesome allegations was preferable to witnessing Raj's humiliation. 'I need a couple of hours respite.'

Five minutes later, Nick and Cain thumbed down a black cab from outside the Victorian hospital.

A discarded anorexic edition of the Evening News had been left in the cab. Cain picked it up.

He fully expected to see April's plight splashed across the front page, but she wasn't there. Nor was she on pages three, five, seven and nine.

He finally located three short paras from an agency source rather than crime reporter Matt Stark. An old thumbnail head and shoulders mugshot accompanied the story on page eleven. The whole incident was underplayed. The result of a scuffle and a tumble rather than a vicious racist assault.

At first glance, he could credit his smart media skills for burying bad news, but he knew better: this was a big story that had been seriously undercooked by people who had a vested interest in keeping it lukewarm.

Progress from Crumpsall into the city's Northern Quarter was slow. He briefed Nick. 'We're going to meet a trash journalist who is threatening to write an expose about three-in-a-bed sex romps.'

'Footballers at it again?'

'Nope.'

'Politicians?'

'Nope.'

'Who then?'

'Me, you and April.'

Nick emitted a rasping hacked cough. 'You're having a laugh.'

'I wish I was. She wants to tell the world about us all shagging each other.' Nick shook his head with subdued mirth. Slapped his thighs. Shared a joke with himself and muttered a few words that Cain could not catch. 'Pardon?'

'I said the missus will do her nut if she thinks I've been fucking around after I promised I would always be faithful.'

'And have you?'

'Do I look like a sex machine?'

It was Cain's turn to laugh inwardly. Nick had a point.

'Our mission today is to stop her submitting her salacious shite. You with me?' asked Cain.

'How are you going to do that?'

'Look mean and nasty.'

'I can do the that.'

The taxi slowly inched its way down Cheetham Hill Road

through the Northern Quarter towards Church Street where the Unicorn stood, a defiant relic of a nostalgic post-war Manchester before the property boom wet dream.

From the back window of the black cab, he looked at his city. Was this the last times he was going to black cab his way around the town?

His DNA was embedded in the bricks and mortar, in the bars and urinals, the football and cricket grounds, the music venues where they sang the story of the blues. The roads and pathways.

He had a story for every street corner. So did his mates and their mates and their mates too. Every Jack and Jill on the pull had dozens of anecdotes to lay on you. Soon as they had a few drinks, everyone was a natural born storyteller.

Cain grinned at the memories. Felt proud of his Manchester, his home where an ugly duckling had become an architecturally significant swan.

Inside the Unicorn society's outcasts nursed alcohol, bonded by the booze and the speed of the sound of loneliness. John Prine's ode to dead romance was on the jukebox as Cain and Nick sauntered in through the door.

He scanned the room to see if June had already arrived. She hadn't.

He ordered himself a pint of bitter. Turned to ask Nick before he double-checked himself. How insensitive to encourage a hard-line alcoholic to partake in alcohol. Then again, it was absurd to expect a man to cold turkey to make him feel better. 'What do you want to drink?'

Before Nick answered, June Hastie entered the pub.

She spotted Cain immediately. Made her way over.

He hadn't seen her in over a decade. Time had not been

kind to her. Her bloated face was flushed red with alcohol abuse. 'Hello June. What do you want to drink? This is Nick Forti.'

'Hi Nick. Large red. Malbec,' said June. Her voice had a boozy smokey rasp.

'Snakebite,' said Nick.

Once they had their drinks, they sat down. Cain expected her to record their conversation. She was a lot more nervous than he remembered.

'Thanks for coming to meet us, June. When we spoke on the phone you made serious allegations about bizarre sex games. You said they involved me, Nick here and April, who is in hospital. Your story is spurious. April was attacked and collapsed in our apartment and…'

'I know,' said June. She sipped her wine twice in quick succession. The hand holding the glass shook. 'I know. I've spiked the story. I was fed duff information about the accident. Really sorry I bothered you. Please accept my apology. Never my intention to intrude on your grief.' She took another two quick sips. The large glass was almost empty. Cain and Nick had barely knocked the heads off their pints.

'Is that it?'

'Yes. Are we finished, Cain? Thanks for the drink.' She downed what was left. Half smiled. Got up to leave. 'Tell your friends we are good. And I've been an obedient June.'

'What do you mean?'

'Been gang banged once against my will, Cain. Don't want it to happen again to me or my daughters. Thanks for the drink.' June placed the glass on the table. Fled the pub. Cain followed her out, leaving Nick minding their pints. He quickly caught up with her. Asked her to stop. Offered her a hundred quid. 'Don't want your money,' she said.

'You're not a quitter.'

'They cannot reach me in Alaska. Nor you in California. Everyone knows you're running scared. Don't blame you, I am too. Got some holiday due. Visit my sister.'

'Did Billy McGinty speak to you direct?'

'A woman.'

'I am sorry.'

'Don't be. My life all over,' said June.

'Who was your source for the story?'

'No chance. Good luck Cain. You'll need it. Sorry about April. Should have stuck to the cooking.'

'Names…?'

Before he had a chance to talk more, she flagged a black cab.

Back in the bar, Cain grabbed his pint and took a few quick gulps.

'Did she tell you owt?'

'No.'

'Welcome to King Bill's dog-eat-man world,' said Nick.

'Why would Billy McGinty protect my name?'

'Don't flatter yourself,' said Nick. 'Billy's cleaning up after Ryan.'

'What should I do?'

'Nothing. Have a drink. Don't get involved.'

'But I am involved. They almost killed April. Could have maimed me. Beat you to a pulp.'

'You're still breathing. You want to keep it that way without provoking Billy.'

'If he wants the points that bad, he can have them.'

Did Cain really believe that? He didn't have the nerve to tell Nick that he was planning to permanently stay six thousand miles away. He'd seen Nick fight twice and each time he'd rather have died than stop boxing.

Cain admired that bravery and felt embarrassed by his own selfish pragmatism. But then again, he didn't have the knock-out punch that Nick could call upon when the chips were down. To have that power would be awesome.

Twenty-Three.

In theory, he had 36 hours to put his affairs in order and say a short goodbye to Manchester.

While he had not officially said yes, he hadn't said no either. His new benefactors had assumed California was nigh on impossible to resist.

Were they right?

He didn't know and there was no one to ask except Little Miss Red Dress. And she was keeping her opinion to herself as Cain and Nick walked slowly down a crowded Market Street towards Deansgate.

The mobile rang. Rita Rock again. She wanted to know if he was finally free to meet up to give a statement and formally identify their attackers.

He stonewalled her again and said he was at the hospital waiting on test results. The time wasn't right today. Swore he would call her tomorrow without telling her it would likely be from Manchester International Airport. Like Raj, she would be disappointed, but how was he meant to react?

He'd just seen a terrified June Hastie drop her threesome

story like a hot potato. Who had dobbed her into McGinty? He'd only told two trusted mates about her press enquiry, Matt Stark and Vince Crane. One was briefing against him, maybe both.

The mobile rang again. A transatlantic call from Hal Rogers. Cain held the phone away from his ear.

Half of Market Street could earwig the one-way conversation.

Even Nick laughed at the over enthusiastic American who said he was looking forward doing great things together.

Best endorsement he'd ever received from Bob. Hal wished him and April godspeed on their journey. Told Cain straight not to worry about the green card. He had connections right to the top. The very top, with the greatest leader that was making the USA great again.

'You definitely going on holiday then?' asked Nick when Cain explained to him Bob's offer.

'What would you do?'

Nick shrugged and cracked his knuckles on his left hand and then his right and then did it again. 'Whatever is best for you and what is best for April. A holiday until it all blows over makes sense.'

'Am I running from Billy McGinty by pretending to help someone who is already dead? Don't answer the question. It's rhetorical.'

'What does that mean?' asked Nick.

'I am not expecting an answer. The question is a figure of speech.'

'You know what, Cain, no one likes a smart arse,' said Nick.

They crossed Cross Street. Took a short cut through

St Ann's Square. Before Cain could think of anything approaching a witty response the mobile rang yet again. Rachel Roberts was on the other end.

'I am holding an online auction. Text me your best offer.'

'For what?'

'Tapes of April sessions.'

'Who else is involved in the auction?'

'That would be telling. Would not make commercial sense as the tapes will go to the highest bidder.'

'Don't be silly, Rachel.'

'Text me your bid within the next hour. May the best man or woman win.'

'Give me a taster of what's on offer?' he asked.

'April knows the truth about Ted Blake.'

'Rachel…' The line went dead. He called her back. Went through to voicemail. 'Don't auction any tapes. You don't understand what you're doing. I'll outbid anyone.'

'What was all that about?' asked Nick.

'Somebody's trying to make a killing,' said Cain, unsure what to do next. He'd never been involved in blackmail before or was it bribery? Or was it a simple commercial transaction?

He plucked the figure of ten grand as his spend on the tapes. It was a big enough sum to grab anyone's interest who only received PAYE or self-employed income.

He called Rachel five times before they reached the apartment block.

Each time he went straight to voice message.

Each time he asked her to call him soon as she could. Important they talked as soon as possible.

In the apartment Bob and Summer had returned from

the hospital. They watched a movie on Apple TV. Played with their mobile Apple device.Threw pizzas and garlic bread down their throats. A large helping of grief hadn't dampened their appetites.

They offered Nick and Cain uneaten congealed triangles. Bob was drinking red wine and offered them both a glass. Said it was a particularly good Merlot, unusual to have decent wine in cursed Manchester, still banging on about how unlucky the city was.

Summer reported there was no change in April. The plan was still to transfer her to the USA for post-op rehab. There was no mention of whether she was actually still alive or not.

Cain didn't want to ask when it was easier to pretend what they were doing was right. Raj could complain all he wanted, but the decision had been made.

Bob asked if Hal had been in touch. Cain said he had and then excused himself and Nick rather than replay the manic conversation with the movie mogul.

They went straight into the office Cain shared with April and logged onto the iMac.

Cain entered the passwords for the online business accounts for the Red Manifesto and waited for admission.

The business had all his spare cash. The two hundred grand he had invested had been swallowed up on brand development and the launch costs.

They could not afford his full-time wages as a marketing director, so he worked for Global Manchester during the day and helped out in the evenings when he had the time.

He thought they had more money in the business. Didn't think the current account overdraft was as high or as permanent. They were two grand off their limited on business account 1 and seven on business account 2. His savings account didn't have much savings in them and there wasn't any sign of Bob lending the business cash over the last six months.

If he wanted to make a bid for the tapes, he would have to raid the wages, tax and VAT account and that could cause all sorts of future untold problems with staff and HMRC. That was the only account with any decent money in it, but it was spoken for. Forty percent of the daily take went into the account to cover overheads and stock and tax. Not that dipping into it bothered him in the remotest.

The future is unwritten, he said to himself as he started the online transfer into his personal account. The phrase was the title of a rock documentary about a dead punk rocker.

He pictured Joe Strummer smoking a fag on the front cover of the documentary about the late Clash singer, who had died of a congenital heart defect at the young age of fifty.

They — whoever they were — could have fun chasing the cash when he was sitting pretty on a beach in California and April was recovering by his side.

He checked the transaction ticked all the right boxes. Everything was in order. He pressed the button to confirm the movement. Text flashed on the screen. Said he didn't have permission to transfer the cash.

'Shit.'

'What's up?' asked Nick.

'Nothing,' replied Cain as he cancelled the transaction and started again, double checking his every entry and movement.

It was the same result the three times he tried.

He was blocked from his own business and his two hundred grand investment. Each time he was told to speak to the account holder. 'Something's wrong.' But he didn't know what it was. April had always handled the money in the business so perhaps it was perfectly normal for him not to be recognised as having admin rights to his own money.

He was annoyed at the inconvenience although it would get sorted out easily enough once he could speak to the bank and explain what had happened to April. Pity they hadn't planned for a contingency if one of them was incapacitated. The arrogance of relative youth thinking you'd live forever, even if you had been knocking at the door. Cain needed another no-fuss, no-questions alternative that would give him immediate access to hard cash.

He looked around the home office for inspiration and saw another dead celebrity wrapped in a thick woolly cardigan giving him the eye from a beach in Santa Monica in North Hollywood.

Norma Jean only made it to 36 before she took her own life, or had it taken from her by assailants unknown.

George Barris had captured Marilyn's zeitgeist with his stills, in the same way Bob Ord had depicted Madchester's hedonistic drug culture by telling the story behind the creation of Rolling Stones' *Exile on Main Street*.

He could dip into the petty cash that April kept in the office safe. She said it was good to keep a float handy, in case of emergencies. And this qualified as one.

'Close your eyes,' said Cain, semi-seriously to Nick who had plonked himself in April's chair and was flicking aimlessly through dull business magazines about the hospitality industry.

Cain removed a photographic print of Monroe. Stared at her rare beauty. April was just as beautiful, a darker skinned, black haired version ten years older than the allegedly lonely star of *Some Like It Hot*.

Behind the most glamorous 21st century icon was a safe. He entered the password. Grabbed the cash in the safe. 'You any good at counting?' asked Cain.

'I can count to eight, then you have to get on your feet or else,' said Nick. He feigned the whites of his eyes rolling in the back of his head as if he had taken a knock-out blow and then remembered what had happened to April. 'Sorry, mate. Slipped my mind.'

'No worries,' said Cain. 'Let's count.'

Although the bundles of money were clearly marked with the amounts written on bits of paper under rubber bands, it took them longer to count than anticipated. Any loss of concentration and they would have to start again.

Midway through, Cain asked him about the Mike Tyson quote and how everyone had a plan until they got punched in the mouth.

The cash counting stopped, while Nick explained that fighting was all about confidence. The more you practised and trained, the more confidence you'd have, irrespective of the power and skills of the boxers.

'Nobody gets lucky and lands a knock-out blow with his eyes shut. Technique and aggression help, but you got to believe that you can hurt people.'

'Do you believe that?'

'Two hundred per cent I can. Still have the force, but not the same will or the 'Boom-Boom'.'

'Does McGinty have it?' asked Cain.

'More than any man I know. Let me show you some tips.'

They sparred briefly.

Nick showed him how to keep both feet planted on the ground while rotating his feet, hips and body and throwing lefts and rights.

Explained how to exhale as the punch was thrown. And indicated the best spots to hit for maximum KO results: the jaw, behind the ear, the temple.

He said the latter was particularly effective because of the lower bone density compared to other areas of the skull. Punches landed there can easily impact the brain. Make opponents dizzy — or even kill them. Or her.

The pair of them had shadow boxed themselves into a repeat brain damage faux pas. The impromptu masterclass session was over. They went back to the counting.

Still distracted, Cain did five counts.

He constantly pictured hitting Swastika Boy. He knew they had known how to hurt April and had not pulled their punches. They had hit her so hard they literally stopped her brain from functioning. They were going to get away with it because nobody had the balls to challenge King Cock, Bill McGinty.

Finally, he announced to Nick they had twelve grand and a few notes in cash.

He didn't know if it belonged to her or the business. He knew it didn't belong to him. He had to make a decision.

He texted Rachel Roberts: 12 grand cash — you can have it now. Tell me where you want to meet?

Was it enough? He would have to see how she responded to the offer. Told him yes or no or asked him to up the bid.

In his eyes, it was very generous. He would pay what he

could lay his hands on — and could envisage doubling his bid.

His friends would be good for the cash if he had a whip round. But he had to wait. Just like Swastika Boy and Scarface had to wait for a signal from the Red Manifesto so they would know when to appear from under Bridge 100 just as he and April approached.

They could hit them knowing Vince was not going to be there because someone had called them.

He could easily find out who was doing what in the Red Manifesto. They had cameras. They had timelines. They could create a narrative based on evidence. 'Want to swap roles? I'll teach and you learn?' asked Cain. 'Pull up a seat next to mine.'

Nick did as he was told.

Cain exited from the online banking site and logged onto the CCTV dashboard where Red Manifesto's security cameras recorded everything. He called up the footage from nine cameras.

Each camera appeared in a three-by-three grid on the large 27' iMac.

He explained the cameras were there to protect staff and customers from violence and theft and not to snoop or pry.

They kept the video footage for eight weeks and then archived the material in case somebody needed it retrospectively.

'One of your jobs at the Red Manifesto will be to monitor the CCTV security system to make sure everything is running smoothly. Follow what I am doing on screen. This is from the night we were attacked,' said Cain, unsure what he wanted to find when he viewed the footage.

'OK,' Nick nodded, his eyes concentrated on the screen, his body leaned towards the powerful iMac.

Cain casually moved the wireless mouse to navigate around the dashboard and clicked on different screens as he explained what part of the restaurant was covered by each camera.

He said they didn't normally look at the screens unless they were resolving issues about payments or staff behaviour. 'This is five minutes to midnight when we were kicking people out. Here is me and Vince talking at the bar. The cougar joined in the conversation, a bit of bored posh who married money,' said Cain.

He looked at her closely and then backtracked her movements across the nine screens until she paid her bar bill on till 7 at 11.12pm. 'This system is so smart. You can marry the footage with the entries to the till and identity transactions and card owners.'

Cain wrote the times down and entered the EPOS system that were the eyes and ears of every cash and stock movement within Red Manifesto.

He entered the terminal number and the time details and waited for the till receipt to pop up: Molly Hawkins had bought a diet coke the entire evening from when she entered at eight until she left shortly before midnight with her love action in tow. 'Typical cheapskate. Noshes on free grub and claps enthusiastically throughout the presentation and buys a single drink.'

'That's because she's barnstorming,' said Nick.

'She's what?'

'Pinching drinks. Look.' Nick took the mouse and tracked Molly as she floated past a group of four women standing by a stone pillar. She put an empty glass down on a shelf. Picked up a full one when nobody was looking, apart from the CCTV. 'Can spot a professional barnstormer a mile off. They are skilled operators. Like women rubbing up against pissed up blokes in pubs and robbing them. Look at the tall red-haired bint? Another one at it.'

Cain followed the cursor on the screen at Nick shadowed Rachel Roberts half inching a glass of wine in a similar scenario to Molly's. Moments later, Molly and Vince were chatting like best friends. Vince said he'd never met her before. Nor could he remember her name.

He took the control of the mouse and forwarded towards the end of the night, when Molly 'propositioned' Vince and pretended to pick him up.

Just before she excused herself to powder her nose, Vince deftly slipped her something when Cain's back was turned.

Could be anything. A mobile number. Drugs. Details of a Chinese takeaway.

'The barnstormer. Can you zoom in on her?' asked Nick.

'Why?'

'Try and get her face on screen and enlarge it.'

'Why?'

'I know her. Or knew when she was a young lassie. Comes from up our way in Radcliffe.'

'You do?'

'One of Gina's Saturday Night Girls,' said Nick.

'Saturday Night what?'

'Good time girls who like to let their hair down. Hang round famous people and shag or blow them.'

'Like you?'

'Like me,' grinned Nick. 'What's her name?'

'Molly Hawkins, according to the credit card she used for her diet coke,' said Cain. 'I'd like to speak to her. Would your ex still know her?'

'Don't know.'

The mobile rang. It was Rachel Roberts. 'My highest bid is double yours at the moment. Two hours to smash it. Cash.'

'Too short notice,' he replied.

'You know April was going to lend me big money to start a business abroad. Did she ever mention it to you?' asked Rachel.

'No.'

'An interest free loan. You sure she never said anything?'

'Nothing.'

'Fuck her and fuck you. Double your bid.' She sounded cokehead desperate, not that Cain knew about drugs. Life was complicated enough with drink without adding Class A to the mix. Before he could think of a response, the line went dead. Could he lay his hands on another twelve grand?

'What happened?' asked Nick.

'I am either being mugged by a cokehead or I am going to find out the truth about April.'

'You could always ignore her. Call her bluff?'

'If you don't want to speak to your missus, you could Google Molly. You know how to use the computer?' asked Cain. Much as he wanted to park Rachel Roberts where the sun didn't shine, she had him hooked.

'Just because I am brain damaged, doesn't mean I am stupid,' replied Nick.

'See what you can find about Molly Hawkins. I am going to ask a man about for a loan?'

'At this time of night?'

'Don't worry. He's sat next door watching my telly, eating my food and controlling my business. I'd like to chat with Molly.'

'Why?'

'Because even if the truth hurts, it still matters,' said Cain.

Twenty-Four.

'What's going on?' asked Cain as he entered the living room. Bob and Summer had guilt written all over their faces.

They were sprawled on separate sofas watching the mega television plonked above a fake fireplace.

At least they weren't sat inappropriately on the same sofa.

Cain checked out the screen to see what they were viewing.

Didn't recognise the action on the telly. But he did notice the workings on the coffee table. Was it Bob, Summer or both of them?

'Want some?' asked Summer. 'Takes the edge off a shit day.'

'No thanks. I'd rather have access to my money in my business. Do either of you know anything about it?'

Summer shook her head. Bob nodded his slowly, drunkenly, a large crystal tumbler in his hand. He had helped himself to the drinks cabinet without asking, like he owned the place. 'What's the problem?' asked the film financier.

'I can't move any money around the Red Manifesto. Do you know why I can't?'

'Way the business is set up.'

'What do you mean?' asked Cain.

'Simple, it's my money that set up the business with a bit of yours thrown in to give you equity because April wanted you to profit from any sales of the brand name. But that is all you've got any stake in. The name. Not the bricks and mortar or the fixtures or fittings. Not the stuff that costs real dosh. You're not getting shares and stock just because you can do a bit of marketing and write a few bloody press releases.'

'Has April stitched me up?'

'Actually, she's done you a favour. Your money is ring fenced so you can never lose it, but you cannot access it unless you sell your stake.'

Cain sat down on a sofa. Felt the crushed leather cushions surrender to his weight. He thought the Red Manifesto was created out of his and April's love for each other.

How wrong could he be? It was just another business transaction.

Looked around the room for Little Miss Red Dress. Needed an ally. She wasn't there. Her appearances were getting more erratic. 'How much of my business do you own?'

'Most of it. If April passes, maybe you two hooking up in the USA isn't such a bad idea after all. Simply exchange an older model for a younger model.'

'You bastard.' Cain moved towards the older man. Summer blocked his path.

Her face was blotchy and eyes red. Maybe from the coke.

Maybe from crying. She had that belligerent look that April had when she was annoyed by an injustice, perceived or real.

'He's pulling your plonker. Teases us both. It's his way, that's all.'

'Of course, I am jesting. It is just my black humour. Comes from working in the film business. The amorality of the place still takes me by surprise. People want fame and fortune so much, yet don't realise the cost they have to pay.'

'Do you?'

'Why do you want money?' asked Bob.

For a beat or two, Cain thought he might have connected with the old man's heart. Did he tell him the real reason or spin him a story? If he did the latter, he was just as devious as they were. 'I might get some information as to why April was attacked.'

'Who from?'

'I am sworn to secrecy,' said Cain.

'You don't want to go there, Cain, believe me. It is too upsetting, even for a man as strong and determined as me,' said Bob. He swirled his liquor around his crystal glass and then sank it one large gulp. Held out his glass to Summer who was still stood up blocking Cain's path to her father. 'You want to hear the truth?'

'Yes.'

'You have to swear on the bible that what I tell you in this room, stays in this room. Go get your bible, Summer.'

After she handed him his refill, she did as she was told. Came back with a holy bible with gold lettering on the front.

'I am atheist,' said Cain. He glanced around the room to see if Little Miss Red Dress had sneaked in unseen. She hadn't.

'So am I,' said Bob, 'I am hedging my bets, in case we're both wrong. Put your hands on the cover and say some words.'

'I want to hear this as well,' said Summer.

'Now is not the time,' said Bob. 'Bring me the bottle, first.'

'But.'

'But nothing …the bottle, then scoot. I'll see you in the morning.'

Summer looked ready to contest the decision to exclude her from the conversation and then she decided to give in.

She shrugged and made her way out of the room towards the bedrooms.

When she had gone, Bob invited Cain to sit down. 'I am telling this because you're leaving Manchester and you should have closure from this cursed city. So let me tell me story without interruptions and no questions. This is my truth, no matter how much it hurts me and what you think of April when I've finished.'

Middle of the nineties I was doing all right. Me, a lad from Salford who left school with nowt but a shrewd mind about how to make money and have a good time.

But it took me a while to get going. I was a printer for ten years, learning a trade and hoping one day to start my own print shop. Married with a couple of young girls living in Eccles.

Then the revolution started up with the e-generation popping pills like the world was on fire. Boring old safe me working 9-5 broke free and started making money out of Madchester, selling posters and t-shirts featuring the Roses and the Mondays and the Carpets … New Order and Cheerful Division … Chameleons and the Charlatans ... all them bands that the kids went mad over.

I was having a ball. I was a dozen or so years older than the kids in the bands who knew I was good with money like a friendly uncle. They asked my help with funding their music videos. I agreed as long as I could protect my money by acting as co-producer. They were all a bit thick and readily agreed.

About this time, I hooked up with April. Love at first sight job. She wanted to help me sell stuff at a Heaton Park gig with Oasis. Ditched me wife and kids and suddenly me and her were an item, Mr and Mrs Manchester, money in our pockets with creativity to burn, rutting like rabbits fuelled by whatever stimulants we could lay our hands on.

Cut a long story short, she got pregnant with twins, a boy and girl, and about the same time I was putting together finance for a film about drugs and hedonism and lots of sex and rock and roll.

Me and this director came up with the idea of focusing on the Rolling Stones at their most hedonistic and musically interesting, which was when they were making Exile on Main Street. Our clever plan was to use the guys in the Manchester bands as Keef, Jagger, Billy, Charlie and Mick Taylor. Appeal to two markets and two generations simultaneously. Brilliant idea, if I say so myself.

We re-recorded all the songs and had a brilliant dead funny script for 'Exile'. Mancs playing Londoners and putting on mockney accents was a hoot. Bez was as gifted as Wyman, Brownie was a spit for Keef and a deadpan Ryder captured Charlie Watts to a tee. Burggie had to make do with Jagger even though he looked much more like Brian Jones.

We wanted to it to be dead authentic too, so we mirrored

the Stones by making it as close to the Villa Nellcôte in the South of France as we could. We hired a villa 60-minutes drive from Nice overlooking over the most brilliant man-made lake in the world.

We had a two-month shooting schedule starting in July that was fast and furious. April was due at the tail end of September so you can imagine she was heavily pregnant with twins when we were finishing the shoot. But she was a team player so you can imagine she was getting stuck in helping with wardrobe and the catering and doing lots of running around for us. Difference with a movie and a video was you knew the costs of the latter.

The former was like trying to tame wild horses. Bloody hard work. Grafting 24/7 and spending 24/7 ... our daily drug budget cost more than a pop video.

Bloody nuts it was. I was working me nuts off through the summer of 97, mindful that I had to make sure April didn't do too much. But you know what she is like.

Thing is, she was pretty robust and healthy and none of us were worried about her. I thought it would be like my first two. They popped out between print runs without me noticing. The ink barely had time to dry before I was knee deep in nappies.

But I am digressing ... I was busy getting the filming finished as we only had the location until the end of August and April went to the hospital for a routine check-up.

One of the crew drove her when it should have been me. She hadn't been feeling too brilliant, but we thought nothing of it.

Then I get the call from the crew member who had driven her to the hospital.

There was a problem with one of the twins and they'd had to do an emergency caesarean. I rushed down there fast as I could. Drove like a lunatic. Happiest day of my life. Worst day of my life.

Next to a sleeping April was the most beautiful little baby girl, a month early but really healthy, according to the medical staff as we communicated through broken English. My French was shite. Still is.

I asked them was the other baby with my little girl, my little boy, my heir apparent.

They said no. I should have guessed but I didn't want to consider anything was wrong even though they were a month early.

Bob took another large drink. Talked to the mid-distance. His words slurred, as if he was on a mission to polish off the bottle before he got to the end of his story.

The liquor watered down with rivers of tears that cascaded down the old man's face.

Cain had guessed the ending, like he did whenever he watched crime movies or read thrillers. He kept his own mouth shut and waited for the reveal.

My baby boy was stillborn. Didn't make it out of the womb alive. Never stood a chance.

They didn't know when he died or how, but it must have been sometime between the scan in Manchester before we left for France and the scan in the hospital in Nice.

I asked if I could see the baby and they said no, it would not be appropriate because of the level of deterioration. If I saw the baby's decomposed remains, it would haunt me the rest of my life, they said.

They were the worst 24-hours of my life. We didn't ask too many questions.

Simply wanted to get away from the smell of disinfectant and the stench of premature death.

We discussed it briefly for five minutes in the car park before we drove back to the villa. Said we would never mention the still-born baby. Be our secret. Would be too heavy a load for Summer to cope with if she ever knew that she had survived while her twin had died. Who knew how that would mess with her head?

April agreed.

There was no funeral. No time to grieve or say goodbye. We signed some papers and then we were on our way. I had a film to finish so a friend drove April back to Manchester with Summer.

I wanted her to stay but she demanded she went home. Said the set was cursed, so I let her go and threw myself into finishing off the shoot as quickly and painlessly as possible.

Should have gone with her but everything we had was invested in that film and I was a dumb ass.

I play tough and pretend I am bullet-proof, but I am just another arsehole who messed up the money. Every single penny. Re-mortgaged the house. Sold my cars. We're driving around in the cheapest hire cars we could afford. Maybe, if I'd gone back with her, we'd have had a chance of keeping our marriage going? I don't know.

The movie was the launchpad for my success in movies but was also the beginning of the end of me and April. She was never the same after we lost our boy. I think deep down she blamed me for it although we never talked about losing the boy.

We split up pretty quick.

She was meant to accompany me to do the PR for the film, but she declined.

Said she needed time by herself and went off travelling

around the globe for years on end, leaving me literally holding the baby whilst playing at being a mega movie mogul.

'She never told me any of this,' said Cain, breaking Bob's no-interruption rule.

He didn't appear to notice. Was this her big secret? It wasn't her fault.

Why would he hate her for having a still-born baby. That made no sense.

And he could hardly blame her for not discussing her loss with anyone. He'd done the same with Hannah. Maintained dumb pig shit ignorant radio silence. Did sweet FA while his wife, drowned in grief. Took off down under. Never to return.

'Me and you have a lot more in common than you ever think, don't we Cain? Both grieving fathers. Living with loss. Never having a chance to come to terms with our loss. You with Hannah. Me with Eric,' said Bob.

'Eric?'

'Cantona, wasn't my idea. Never understood football. You know I never stopped loving her. The hurt never left her, but she was finally happy when she met you. Told me you had dreams for the restaurant. That's why I helped. Pulled a few strings and called in a few favours from old friends, who owed me a drink or two. Gave her a chance to recover in the USA with you and her daughter by her side. A chance for me to pay her back properly.'

'Why did you keep it secret?'

'We made a mistake. Regretted it ever since,' said Bob.

'It was nobody's fault. That's the big difference between you and me. I never got closure when the bastard drove into my daughter and broke her neck. There was no justice when the bastard stopped. Looked at what he done and then drove off again. I had to suffer in the dark for six months before I got a name and a very thin slice of poetic justice when a roadie called Ted Blake apparently confessed. And then twenty years later, April, out of the blue, claims he wasn't the man. He was lying. Do you know anything about that? Is there anything else you want tell me?' asked Cain. 'Did you know Ted Blake? He roadied for the Rolling Stones? Maybe moved in your circles too?'

Bob's eyes had turned with the alcohol. Spun slowly around his skull. Cain's questions remained unanswered.

Bob had nodded off. During his monologue, he had refilled his tumbler several times. Three inches were marooned at the bottom of the bottle. The rest swilled around his body. Poisoned his blood.

The crystal glass tumbler was gripped loosely in his hand. Then it wasn't. It spilt on the expensive suede sofa, not that the price of furniture mattered at a time like this.

Did Cain believe his confession? Should he take it at face value? Why would a man lie about such as tragic situation?

In reality, there were any number of reasons. Ted Blake had been a dying man when he spoke to Cain and Len Harvey on his deathbed.

If Ted lied, why wouldn't Bob.

He should help him out, but he was not his responsibility. That was his daughter's and he knew exactly where she would be, on the other door earwigging. He would have done the same.

To prove he was right in his assumption, he jerked open the living room door quickly.

Summer almost fell on top of him. She stumbled and quickly straightened herself up. 'I had a brother, a dead twin I never knew about. A boy called Eric. There was no shame. I could have handled it. But not to know. Never to be told. That's cruel. How could they never have told me? Him and her?'

'I never knew. Your mum never told me. Swear blind. I am too exhausted to think about it now, but we can talk in the morning. Only us. I swore confidentiality.'

'You don't believe in swearing on oath so your words mean nothing,' said Summer.

'You're right,' he said. Little Miss Red Dress was stood behind her, mouth zipped. Cain was unsure what more to say to a young woman who had just discovered she had a dead still-born twin. Would she remember his Ted Blake riff? He doubted it. 'He's fast asleep in there, mid-conversation. But you heard it all? Wake him and help put him to bed. He might have continence issues. If you want to talk ...'

'If my God can't help me, I'll knock on your bedroom door and you can lend me a helping hand or I can give you one,' said Summer, without a hint of irony and opened the lounge door. 'A helping hand with the packing, obviously.'

Cain nodded towards Little Miss Red Dress to let her know lewdness was not appreciated.

He entered his office and was surprised to find a black man on his computer watching movies. He had been so wrapped in Bob's revelations he'd forgotten all about Nick.

He hoped he wasn't watching porn and having a tug. 'You going to be long?'

'Been busy people watching on your CCTV footage from inside the Red Manifesto.'

'Find anything else out?'

'Yes. Your man Vince uses your restaurant to deal big time and our posh Saturday Night Girl Molly Hawkins hooks.'

'How can you tell that from a computer screen?'

'Your telephone. Called the wife. She told me Molly was a part-time barmaid and actress before she became a full-time masseuse.'

'You spoke to your wife?'

'Yes.'

'Bet you she was pleased for a call after midnight.'

'She works the graveyard shift in a care home. Pays better than day work. Her mum looks after the kids with my sisters stepping in. Told her I was living in the tallest, poshest building in Manchester.'

'That's good,' said Cain. He could see Nick felt the same. He looked different from the pisspot guitar hero who rescued him and April. 'You going to speak to her again?'

'She's going to do some detective work for me. I told her how you helped me.'

'I've done nothing.'

'That's still more than anyone else. You've not judged me,' said Nick.

'What's she going to do?'

'Tell us where Molly Hawkins lives or works. She thinks she works in Pandora's Box in Tib Street, but she's going to confirm it in the morning.'

Alone in his bedroom with Little Miss Red Dress, Cain looked out over the sleeping city as the drunks and drugged and the shagged and shaggers, hailed black cabs or bedded down in doorways, sheltering from the cold night breezes blowing up Deansgate.

Bob's story was printed out on a couple of sheets of A4. Although he would try to corroborate it as much as possible, he didn't have time to play wicked games with nut jobs.

He placed Bob's script on the floor and curled up into a ball on the bed.

Grabbed April's pillow and held it to his chest so he could smell her smell.

He had never felt more relaxed than when the two of them were bare in each other's arms.

Time would stand still as they drifted on the oceans of physical compatibility.

But it had been fake.

Poor April, the most beautiful woman in the world, hid the most terrible secret from him.

When they were intimate, he would often run his fingers over the thin white caesarean scar on her podgy abdomen before they went lower.

An innocent loving gesture must have been sheer torture, but he had never known. She hadn't loved him enough to tell him the truth. All that imagined simpatico was exactly that: imagined.

'All pretend, the whole bloody charade was one big fake. We were never happy, not real happiness.'

'No, it wasn't Daddy. You're just worried about everything. April. Me. The past. The future. Now.'

'At least you were happy the short time you were with us.'

He smiled at Little Miss Red Dress sat in the semi-dark moonlight on the chaise long in the bedroom where April would normally neatly stack her clothes before she changed into her nightwear. Happy Little Miss Red Dress kept him sane, mad as her existence was.

Twenty-Five.

'Should I stay or should I go?' Cain looked at his face in the mirror and didn't have a clue what to do when his bruised reflection looked bleakly back at him, unable even to raise a smile.

A few nights earlier April had been stopped breathing on the bathroom floor. No wonder he could not crack a grin.

Had April banged her head on the sink unit? An accident after a kerfuffle but was not the cause of her head injury.

They would never know. Never. Because nobody was there when she fell.

He showered, shaved and scrubbed himself to avoid the breakfast table.

The late-night revelations had muddied the waters. Summer had a secret still-born twin brother.

He played for more time as he counted the money on the loo.

He'd never had that much money in his hands in cash in his life. Didn't seem much packaged in fifties. Just a normal wedge for the entrepreneurial wheelers and dealers who loved the risk taking. For most it was a three-or-four-months wages, a sum not to be sniffed at even if most of it would find its way up Rachel Roberts' nose. Should he give her the money and appeal to her conscience?

He put the money back in the large brown manilla envelope and left the en suite. He was only going to wind himself up if he carried on playing in the quicksand.

He needed to be doing rather than thinking. 'Nick?'

'Yes.'

'We're going out in five,' said Cain.

He popped his head around the corner where Bob and Summer ate their breakfasts in sullen silence. He told them he had to run a few errands and tie up some loose ends. He'd text when he knew his timeframe for the day.

Five minutes later they marched down Deansgate like evangelists selling Jesus. 'Walk don't think.'

'What?' asked Nick.

'Talking to myself,' said Cain.

They tried the gym where Rachel Roberts worked out. She wasn't there. They tried her office. It was still locked. They tried her flat in the Northern Quarter. There was no answer. Cain held the brown envelope. Behind the locked doors there was a row of letterboxes.

'You're going to piss away twelve grand?'

'Yes.'

'You're crazy.'

'Not my money. I must know before I go.'

'That was more than my last purse. Ten grand. After expenses I had two left. A mug's game. It's too hard to earn to throw it away.'

Ten minutes later Cain had done just that. A female

resident had left the apartment block to go to work. The two of them entered in her slipstream. Placed the money in Rachel Roberts' letterbox. Cain had written on the envelope: half now, the rest later when you give me the info. Leaving UK in 24 hours. Don't let me down. 'Where did your missus say Molly Hawkins worked?'

'Pandora's Box, but she never confirmed it.'

'Call her and check.'

'She's come off the night shift. I am not going to wake her.'

Instead, they walked the short distance to Tib Street and found an old building with a neon sign above the door and blacked out windows. 'What do we do?' asked Cain. He'd never been to a massage parlour sober. On trips abroad it had been part of the crack.

'Ring the bell,' said Nick, 'And smile for the camera. They'll decide if they want to let you in.'

'At 11am?'

'Men want sex 24/7.'

Cain pressed the buzzer and said he was looking for a massage.

He hoped Little Miss Red Dress wasn't watching his embarrassment. The door buzzer went and him and Nick climbed to the top of the stairs.

He tried to play to it cool, although he felt a fool and almost decided confronting Molly wasn't worth the humiliation. If he had more time, he could have arranged for them to meet away from her workplace.

'Been here before, darlings?' asked the receptionist dressed in a white tee-shirt and blue jeans, her hair pulled back tight from her sunbed face.

Without waiting for an answer, she added the parlour had two girls on today.

Cain recognised her straight-away. 'Fifty pounds for half an hour. Two hundred if you want a foursome. Any extras, you negotiate with the girls. Two men of the world like you know the score. Cash or a card?'

Cain looked at Nick as Molly Hawkins described the two girls and skin tones, vital statistics and fifth and sixth form academic achievements. 'What about you?' he asked.

'I am the receptionist. I don't do massages.'

'You can make an exception for me.' She looked at him closely as her sales spiel dried up. Her light blue eyes locked on his for a moment or two while she tried to place him.

Cain could see her doing the sums, the lights flickering. She was completely different from the woman coming onto Vince.

Almost like she was acting out a role, like she was performing another one here as the cheerful sassy receptionist.

His observations were heavily influenced by what Nick had told him about her part-time acting career. He knew she could play a part.

'Fifty?'

He handed her his debit card. She took it without paying it much attention.

Handed him the cash machine to key in his four-digit code. He did as he was told and gave it back to her.

She looked at Nick, who had gone and sat down on one of the sofas and started to leaf through a magazine. 'Just me,' said Cain. 'He's a happily married man. Or wants to be!'

'OK. Give me five minutes,' she said. 'I didn't expect to be in demand this morning.'

She showed Cain into a bedroom with a double bed with a towel on it. Pleasant enough despite the strong smell of baby lotion, rubber and weed. She bent over. Put a plug into the jacuzzi. Turned out the water. Tested the heat was OK. 'Jump in anytime you want. I'll sort out cover for the desk.'

He glanced around the room and hoped Little Miss Red Dress wouldn't be shaming him about being in a room with a hooker. Another time and another place and this would be a great anecdote in search of a great punch line — as long as it did not involve his daughter.

He sat gingerly on the bed and felt guilty for even considering clambering into the water.

Molly came back into the massage room. She had let down her bleach blonde hair. Taken off the tight faded black jeans and white bra. Her breasts swung freely under the thin white t-sheet cotton.

'You've not got in the 'cuzzi,' she said.

'No,' replied Cain, feeling like an embarrassed schoolboy on a date with a much more experienced girl.

Molly shrugged indifferently as if self-consciousness was the norm. 'Some men want a girlfriend experience. Is that what you're after?'

'Not really. We've met before.'

'Have we?'

'You copped off with my head of security at the Red Manifesto restaurant on the night my fiancée was attacked and hospitalised. I've got a couple of questions.'

'You've paid fifty quid. The time is yours. We can get comfortable and then you can quiz me for the full thirty minutes.'

Cain searched the light blue eyes for any sign of emotion.

There was nothing behind them. She smiled. 'Very sorry to hear about your partner. I might have read about it in the paper. Never really pay much attention to news. The media always stitch you up and print lies about you, especially if you're a vulnerable woman with big tits and no voice.'

'Were you working that night?'

'What do you mean 'working'?'

'Do you often pick up strangers in bars, pretending to be somebody you're not? The rich bored Cheshire housewife picking up a bit of rough ... that's not the reality I am seeing now ... But on the night April was...'

'My reality is two hungry strapping lads who want to go to university. Not that anything I do is any of your business. Fifty quid means you can penetrate my body, not my head.'

Cain felt like a typical misogynist. April would have chastised him for his oafish behaviour if he had behaved like that in front of her.

He was saved by a loud double knock on the door. His heart missed a beat.

Was this another impromptu meeting with Swastika Boy and Scarface? Bloody hell, he was about to take a kicking from the poshest, politest scallies in Manchester, who knocked on the door before they beat the shit out of you.

He relaxed as he considered the situation and listened while Molly told whoever was outside to enter.

The door opened. A woman stood there like she owned the place or, at least, was the office manager dressed in a black trouser suit and purple blouse. 'Hello Molly. You must be Cain Bell. Is he giving you a hard time?'

'He's a talker,' grinned Molly.

'I can give you a couple of minutes if you want to puff

'your dust, but forget any suggestions of a threesome.'

'He was more interested in talking about my freelance activities, Violet,' said Molly.

'If you're not going to shag each other, might as well cure his curiosity, Moll. Fire away Cain. Whatever is said in this room, stays in this room.'

'Who are you?' asked Cain.

'I am Violet, Violet McGinty. This is my massage parlour. Molly called me when you popped in with your little black friend, whose wife also called me last night. My ears are red hot with your name popping up all over the place. What has he been asking, Molly?'

The receptionist briefly recapped their conversation prior to the interruption.

Violet listened and repeated her confidentiality clause. 'I am tremendously sorry about what happened to April, a horrific accident…We were close friends once. How is she doing?'

Cain admired her balls. 'If you're as informed as you claim to be, you'll know exactly how she is doing. Whatever happens, she'll never be the same again.'

'My heart bleeds for you both. Hopefully, they can help her in California. If you need any help, you just have to ask me. Me and April were best friends back in the day.'

'Were you?' asked Cain, another secret April had kept from him. Three years living together yet she had never mentioned her friendship with Violet McGinty.

'Am I done here?' asked Molly. 'I'll get dressed and go back on reception.'

'Any more questions, Cain?' asked Violet.

'Why pretend to you and Vince were two strangers?'

'Fantasy role play.'

'I am not getting this?'

Violet intervened. 'Molly was hired to act the posh bored housewife picking up a bit of rough. They shagged in the car out by Elton Reservoir. I arranged it for a watch and wank client and his wife. Simple,' said Violet.

'The CCTV shows you making a call just before you left…?'

'She called me and I called the client. You can go back to work now, Molly. Refund Cain his fifty quid. And thanks for calling me. Always good to clear the air.'

Alone in the room, Violet pulled the plug from the jacuzzi. Tidied up the room. Gave it a quick cosmetic once over. 'Satisfied?'

'Not really,' said Cain.

'Ask me any questions. Like I said, it stays in the room.'

'You won't tell me the truth.'

'You were mugged by a couple of blacks who are impossible to identify. That part of town by the canal is a real health hazard for tourists getting mugged. Word on the grapevine is she banged her head on the bath. You can never tell with tragic accidents like this. A court could never convict anyone with that amount of doubt.'

'You want me to believe that?' asked Cain. 'Do you know something I don't?'

'If I did, I'd tell the police,' she said. 'I used to be an officer and still feel obliged to uphold the law wherever and whenever I can.'

'Would you really?' asked Cain. He felt conned. Vince was a part-time porn stud, fucking to order for rich impotent peeping toms and their sad blue rinse Cheshire wives.

That would be their story. They would stick to it. The black mugger narrative had already been aired by white attackers.

April deserved better than to be the butt of a racist conspiracy. And so did he. 'I will miss her so much if she dies. We were soulmates.'

Violet responded to his muted outcry. She moved to his side. Stroked his arm gently with crimson red nails. He felt an involuntary shiver. Felt disgusted by her overwhelming confidence in her sexuality. April has, or had, the same touch. The same nonchalant ease.

'I am fighting with you, Cain. She's too young to pass. Has too much passion for life. Like me and you, Cain, like me and you and Billy. He's much maligned, but he's a good man too. Limited in terms of his tastes. He would never eat out at your restaurant. Says it is too posh. I am the one who has to suffer because the old man is a luddite. I don't often eat out at nice places. Billy is a two meat and veg man. Apart from his Friday night curry with the lads. He thinks Tapas is foreplay on a Sunday morning. Imagine the thrill of being tapped on your naked backside to see if you want to be poked? You know you don't have the monopoly on grief. Pain isn't exclusive to you. This isn't Manchester's first accidental tragedy and it won't be the last. Not even your first tragedy,' said Violet.

'Nor April's. She told me all about what happened with the still-born baby. She had counselling with Rachel Roberts for years to cope with the loss of Eric,' said Cain. If she could lie, he could be economical with the truth too. Whatever secrets April harboured, he would pretend he knew all about them. 'What pain to lose a child that way. At least I shared ten years with my Hannah. Saw her grow and smile and laugh and scream with happiness. Imagine pulling Eric decomposed remains from the womb. You'd never get over that, would you? Poor rotting Eric. Poor distraught mum.'

Bob's drunken, slurred words about a stillborn had become April's.

Violet's Cool-Hand-Lucy demeanour evaporated. Her legs went from under her. He caught her. Stopped her from collapsing. Guided her gently to the bed. Sat her down. White face drenched in perspiration. A crimson red rash spread across her neck. 'If you ever want to talk about it?' asked Cain, holding her clammy hand. She squeezed so hard, it hurt him.

'I am sorry for April. And I was sorry for Hannah…when she told me about your loss. I understand it one hundred percent. Nothing I can do. If it would do any good, you have to believe, I would help.'

He held her tight. Hugged her in her arms, wrapped around her.

She fitted into him like they were a perfect match. He could feel her warm breath on his face. Smelled of mint and fresh toothpaste.

He looked past her and saw Little Miss Red Dress admonishing him, giving him the full wagged finger.

Then Violet broke the embrace.

Tried unsuccessfully to push his body away from her. Vomited over the two of them. Hurled the contents of her stomach over his body. Retched long and deep from the bottom of her soul. His face and upper body were covered in her puke and he fought hard to stop himself from throwing up himself.

Twenty-Six.

They tidied themselves up in shocked silence. Wiped down soiled clothing with rolls of tissues stacked on wooden shelves to clean up after satisfied punters.

Violet changed the sheets on the bed. Cain sprayed the room with air fresher.

They got on their knees. Picked up carrots dotted amongst brown ming puddled on the floor. He noticed a white caesarean scar above her black pants, identical to April's. Glanced up from her podgy belly. Focused on her face rather than her crotch. She looked anaemic, the wife of Manchester's most intimidating gangster shellshocked.

'I am devastated by what happened to April. She was the kindest, most loving person I've ever met in my entire life. We were like sisters, we were that close.'

'What happened?'

'Grief intervened. The loss of her son in France was too much,' said Violet. 'Summer was not enough.'

'Were you there?'

'We gave birth within 48 hours of each other. Me first

and then her. Caesareans. She had hers because she was carrying the twins and there was a worry about one of them not moving. One kicked on one side but not on the other. Me, because I had a a umbilical cord prolapse where the umbilical cord slipped into my kipper. The cord can get pinched. They were worried Ryan may not get enough oxygen.'

'When were you in France?'

'Bob was shooting his drugs and debauchery Rolling Stones film and we were out on holiday. All hands to the pump because we were on a budget. Pregnancy fitted with the movie's hippy vibe. The film was almost finished when we both gave birth, her on 27 August and me on the 28th. Neither of us had planned caesarians. We had to wait for three days while we recuperated before we could go home. April was in bits. She had lost her Eric, stillborn. Just laid there. You know they didn't even knock her out, the bloody French. A failed injection in the spine. She was awake during the whole bloody shambles. I could hear her next door. The whole of the south of France must have heard her.'

'She never told me,' said Cain.

'Why would anyone want share such an experience?'

A fair point. Hannah had died four and three days after the respective births of Ryan and Summer.

Perhaps that was why April and Cain had clicked. Shared grief city blues. Sonny Liston's guitar, trumpet and bell.

Violet ignored the irony that her son possibly killed her best friend.

Why deny the contradiction and protest his innocence?

The mobile interrupted their temporary truce. Cain glanced at the screen. 'Hello Detective Inspector Rock,' he said, putting the call on speaker so Violet could hear the conversation.

'You avoiding me, Cain? You said you'd pop into the station to identity April's attackers.'

'I've been at the hospital. Difficult for me.'

'The longer this goes on, the less chance we have of getting the evidence we need to secure a conviction. I understand why you might not necessarily trust us after your experiences with Len Harvey all those years ago, but I am different. I've been doing a bit of checking, like I promised.'

'Did you say hello to Len from me?'

'Has dementia. Lives in a care home in Whitefield,' said Rita. 'Used to revere him although we were chalk and cheese. I collected evidence while he relied on snitches.'

'Was he that out of touch? Always seemed kosher to me.'

'Kept extensive notes. A code only he could transcribe. Sadly, I cannot help you with any feedback on your Hannah's car accident. Nothing there apart from an unsubstantiated rumour about a Ted Blake, who died six months after the accident.'

'Thanks for the info,' said Cain.

'I've heard rumours you're leaving town?'

'Only for treatment for April. I've been advised by the best experts that the USA is the best option.'

'Make sure you give us a proper official statement before you leave. Understand?'

'I will,' said Cain. He cut the connection without saying goodbye or thanking the detective for the call.

'Will you give a statement?' asked Violet.

Had she gamed him? Hooked and reeled him? She had been on a mission to find out what he was going to do as much as he had wanted to discover what she knew. But now it was clear.

Any conversation with her was pointless. There was no appealing to her humanity. Violet was never going to drop her son in the deep muddy stuff.

No matter what he had done, she would excuse his behaviour. A young man confused by his identity and his politics.

He was wasting his time, even thinking he could prick her conscience.

Billy would be even worse than her. There was one thing worse than a mother fixated on her son and that was a father who wanted to create a mini version of himself.

He glanced beyond Violet at Little Miss Red Dress, sat in the edge of the jacuzzi looking pretty upset and nodded at her.

Violet followed his eye line, noticed the nod. 'You OK? You're acting like there is somebody in the room? Are you seeing people? Imaginary friends?' asked Violet. She laughed at her own question. 'You should go see that counsellor, Rachel Roberts. Everyone else does. Better confess to her than the police. You really don't want to be talking to them.'

He stood up and turned his back on Violet as he dressed himself. The damp clothes were superficially clean.

For one of few times in his life, he wasn't searching for a killer punchline.

Whatever he said would fall on deaf and dumb ears, so he fired from the hip. 'Your son and his scar-faced partner, your brother Liam, have already told me what happens if I talk to the police. They have a fondness for knives, don't they?'

'You have an affection for cold steel too,' said Violet. She brushed imaginary creases from her black trouser suit same way Vince Crane did. 'Your decision to leave Manchester is a smart move. Same as your decision not to hurt Ted Blake was the right one too. Ted was popular. A good egg.'

'He was also innocent,' whispered Cain, unsure if she heard him.

Her head was cocked slightly.

Whatever she knew, she was never going tell. The only person who would spill the beans was her husband, Billy McGinty.

Twenty-Seven.

Only one person knew about the night of the long kitchen knife when Cain had lost all reason.

Only one person and he had sworn blind that he would never tell a soul that Cain Bell had a genuine killer instinct.

According to Rita Rock, Len Harvey had lost his mind and was in a care home in Whitefield.

He was unsure if a man living with dementia was an unreliable witness. There was only one to find out.

Go and ask him.

First, he stonewalled Nick's incessant questions about bonking Molly and Violet. Said he was dead impressed with Cain's stamina. Two women at his age was a considerable achievement, especially when one of the brides was the wife of Manchester's notorious gangster.

'If Billy McGinty knew you were alone with his wife in a massage parlour in your boxers…'

'Not funny,' said Cain, and it wasn't.

'Just banter. Black comedy eases the tension. Don't take yourself too seriously,' said Nick.

Took them an hour and a half to walk the six miles from the Northern Quarter via Cheetham Hill and Prestwich before they reached Whitefield.

Cain avoided the quicker new road in preference to the parallel old road. The shorter route was where Hannah had been killed when she crossed the road. He felt anxious in the centre of Prestwich.

Outside the care home, Nick took up his position. Armed himself with a begging cup and a 'help me' sign. Plonked his butt a hundred yards from the entrance. Since he had rescued Cain and April, they had rescued him back. 'I'll stop you from being jumped by those bloody McGinty bastards if it is the last thing I do,' said Nick. "Boom-Boom' them into next week.'

Inside the home, Cain introduced himself to duty manager Helen Tapody. She invited him into her office. Cain was Harvey's second visitor in less than 24 hours. One of his former colleagues had dropped by earlier this morning.

Cain told a little white lie when he claimed he was Len's nephew who felt guilty neglecting him for so long. 'What can I expect when I see him? Will he recognise me?'

'Len's living with dementia. He's watches TV mostly, but isolates himself from the rest of the care home community.'

'Through choice?'

'His brain is operating at a quarter of the capacity it did in his prime. No nice way of saying it. The old uncle Len you may remember is gone. Replaced with a different one. That's not to say this one is any less happy than the younger version, just different.'

Despite the warning, Cain exhaled deeply when he saw the shell of a former giant, muscle and meat vacuumed off him, his skin hanging off sharp brittle bones. Once alert eyes stared vacantly at a small TV screen in a small room with a small bed and small windows looking out into a small panoramic of small terraced houses. His voice weak and croaky, in stark contrast to the booming foghorn that pronounced he was up for some action.

> *The last time Cain Bell had seen Len Harvey had been in the Black Boy pub on the border of Radcliffe and Whitefield.*
> *'You satisfied now,' Len had asked as he downed a pint in one before ordering another. 'You got your confession and avoided a murder charge. You have closure and you have poetic justice. Just have to forgo seeing his name across the front page of the Evening News.'*
> *Harvey had drunk half a gallon and gone shagging in Piccadilly Gardens to celebrate another satisfied client.*
> *Cain had walked home and felt incomplete. His isolation only passed when April Sands walked into his life in Japan.*

'Hello Lenny. Your nephew Cain is here to see you. He's come all the way from America, haven't you?'

'Hello Len.' Cain nodded. 'You've changed. How old are you now, Lenny?'

'One hundred and fifty.' Harvey looked to the duty manager for conformation. Winked at the Aussie. 'Maybe two hundred.'

'Who is the Prime Minister?

'Ted Heath. Or is it Harold Wilson? Or Mike Yarwood?'

'Is that typical?' Cain asked Helen. She nodded and didn't look surprised at Harvey's answers.

'He still has a sense of humour although he struggles

with words and new memories,' said Helen.

'Who are you again?'

'Cain, Cain Bell. It is good to see you again, Uncle Lenny.'
There was no recognition. Not that he could blame him.
Cain would have struggled to recognise Harvey if Tapody
hadn't said it was him.

'How do I know you?' Harvey asked, after Tapody had
gone.

'We were friends when you the detective of the decade in
Manchester.'

'Was I?'

'Manchester's best detective. Nothing happened without
you knowing about it.'

'Who are you?'

'Your buddy. We used to sink pints down the Dog &
Duck in Shudehill. Played killer darts on Saturdays. You
used to tell me you had eyes and ears on every street corner,
down every gutter and up every drain-pipe.'

'I did?'

'Bet you even knew who bombed the city in '96 when
the IRA were at war with us? They could have killed dozens
of us. Nobody was ever arrested or convicted.'

'Bloody IRA. Not enough evidence. Not the will to
prosecute,' said Harvey. His voice stronger, his eyes shone
brighter for a moment or two.

Had the fog lifted temporarily? Cain only wanted a
couple of answers. 'Same with Hannah Bell, the schoolgirl
who killed in a hit and run in Prestwich the night Princess
Diana died. You remember? You said you knew who the
driver was, but there was not enough evidence to prosecute.'

'Did I?'

'What was the name of the driver? Can you remember? I bet you remember United and Fergie and Cantona. What about the driver of the car?'

'King Eric. I loved his upturned collar. You had a knife. You're the man with the big long carving knife.'

They were getting somewhere. 'Why did I need the knife?'

Harvey looked blankly at Cain and then at the muted TV screen with subtitles. A repeat of the Sweeney was on. They probably thought a senile old detective would enjoy seeing John Thaw beat the crap out of criminals, no questions asked. 'You wanted to kill him?'

'Who did I want to kill and why?' asked Cain. He didn't want to feed the answer to a deflated old man who had once roared with the energy a wild furious grizzly bear.

'Are you Ted? I thought you were dead, Ted?'

'Who, Len, who did I want to use it on?' Cain had to keep him in the moment. 'You were a good officer. Hard but fair. Ask anyone about Len Harvey. Hard but fair. Nobody owned you. You were your own boss. That officer who saw you today. Rita Rock. She said you were the best she ever worked with. Len Harvey. Guitar hero. I was in a massage parlour. Beautiful girl wanted to be remembered to you. Molly was her name. Lovely girl. Molly Hawkins. Used to sing in a band and act on TV before she entertained us in other ways…. What was the songs we liked in the Dog and Duck…Jukebox songs?'

Harvey called out for a nurse in a half whisper. His voice would not carry. There was a red button near the arm of his chair. He reached for it.

Cain got there first. Clasped the red button in his hand.

'We used to drink down the Black Boy as well, me and you. Listening to the Stones and the Who … and Zepp… Our mate was a roadie for the Stones. You remember? Driving back from a gig in Europe he had an accident.'

'Ted. Ted Blake. Poor sod had pancreatic cancer. No chance of surviving.'

'Good boy, Len. Who told you Ted was driving the car? Who was your grass?'

'The film fella, the one who thought he was tougher than he was. Said Blakey 'fessed out of guilt once he had been told he was dying.'

'What was the film fella's name?'

'Bob. Billy Bob Bob. Bob Billy. Silly Billy. Hilly Billy Silly. Will you make me a cup of tea?' asked Harvey. He began to rock gently in the chair, his eyes glazed over and his breathing wheezy.

Cain did as he was asked. Went and made him some tea.

When he returned, he let the detective doze for five minutes while he inspected the old rascal's cell. The room was dotted with photographs.

One stood out. A group shot of fifty or sixty people on the set of *All Down The Line.* Manchester's finest. Younger. Thinner. Hairier. Goofier. Childlike as they posed for the camera. Famous actors. Extras. And the crew. The financiers. The hangers on. Among them a young Bob Ord sandwiched between a thinner Vince Crane and a gaunt Ted Blake. To their left two very pregnant women. April was Summer's spit. Next to her Violet.

And who was the man with an arm casually draped over April's friend's shoulders?

He could hazard a guess, but a man needed to be told.

Guessing was for idiots. 'Len. This picture is great. Never knew you worked in the movies. 'That bloke with the pregnant woman, who is he?'

'Billy, Billy McGinty. Saved the movie. They were skint, but he came up with the cash from his drug dealing. Invited me along to scare the shit out of them union boys making the film. The strong arm of the law was a wiser move than having gangsters fannying about.'

'Did you tell him about me and the knife? Or anyone else?'

'You're the wee girl's pa, the one that was killed in Prestwich … by Ted Blake.'

'That's me. I was going to stab him to death until we fought over the knife. Who did you tell about it? Did you tell Billy?'

'Ask him next time you see him.'

'I've never met him.'

'Course you have, you and him are big time mates. He asked me to take you under my wing when your daughter died. Look after you. Make sure I didn't let you do anything stupid.'

'Did he know who really drove the car.'

'Yes.'

'Who?'

'Ted Blake, dummy. Or was it Mike Yarwood? Silly Billy.'

Twenty-Eight.

Outside the two men walked in silence until they found a coffee shop by the met station.

Cain ordered two coffees. They sat at the back facing the door. They would be able to see anybody entering. Nick added several sugars to the cup and stirred his coffee. 'Did you find what you were looking for?'

A good question.

Harvey was lucid one minute and confused and rambling the next; the once sharp investigative mind trapped in dementia roulette.

Cain was unsure if he had spoon-fed the answers to hear what he wanted to hear. Possibly the same was true of all secrets about to be exposed.

April and himself had pretended to be open about every subject, but they had bottled up horrors throughout their time together.

She had never admitted to a stillborn child. Why did they wear their secrets like badges of shame, unwilling to admit vulnerability?

They weren't any less human for showing weakness under emotional pressure. What did he know? If he hadn't pushed for the ultimate commitment, nothing would have been revealed and they would have carried on living the great lie.

Perhaps Summer and Rachel Roberts were right.

He needed to confide in an actual person rather than imaginary conversations with Little Miss Red Dress. He didn't understand mental illness at all. He had been lucky and had avoided head problems all his entire life. But he did know that if you were ill, you wouldn't necessarily know until an expert pointed it out.

'Bollocks.'

'Pardon,' said Nick.

'When I went to meet Ted Blake, I took a carving knife with me.'

'That was very brave of you,' said Nick. 'Not.'

Cain saw contempt on Nick's face. 'If I had used it I would have been just as bad as Swastika Boy.'

'Worse,' said Nick. 'You know the difference between right and wrong. He doesn't.'

'Ted Blake used to live a mile or so from here. Virtually in my own backyard. Probably drank in the same pubs. Ate in the same curry houses. There is or was a knife on the garage roof. My knife. Wonder if it still there?' asked Cain.

'Would you have used it?' asked Nick. 'Don't like being around knives. Cowards use them.'

'You calling me a coward?'

'Yes.'

'Harvey disarmed me pretty easily.'

'What would you have done with it? Where would you have stabbed Blake? In the chest. The neck. Cut his jugular?

Stabbed him or slashed him. Spliced the arteries on his legs? Just the once or multiple times in a frenzy driven by the desire for revenge?'

'You've never lost a child,' said Cain.

'I lost everything else. My kids don't see me. My wife hates me. Only the drink loved me until I needed it more than I needed my family and my friends. You'll be the same. Best thing to do is to leave Manchester. Start a new life.'

'If April dies?'

'All the more reason to refresh.'

'And so Swastika Boy walks free?'

'You can't compete with knives and guns or an 80 mile an hour Mercedes driven straight at you. Hardest man in the world comes second to a fast car. If you ever meet Billy McGinty, it's one of his standard quips: how hard are you, harder than a speeding Mercedes with me behind the wheel? But that's not you. That's not Cain Bell playing Jack Reacher.'

'How do you know?'

'You're too bright. You know big words. You speak posh. But you don't know what your revenge looks like? What it tastes like? How it smells? You want to become what he is? That's your choice. Like it was mine to carry on shagging despite numerous last chances. How many times did she have to tell me before I listened? Today, I get it. At long last. I am in a brothel surrounded by young available women gagging for my cash and all I wanted was a cup of tea.'

Cain laughed loudly. 'Nick you talk a lot of sense and a load of bull at the same time.'

'Forget that. Was April right or wrong? Was Ted Blake the driver?'

'Len Harvey said he was. Still. Not in a fit state of mind to lie, so he must have believed what the film fella told him.'

'Bob Ord?'

'Film fella could mean anyone on the set.'

'Why don't we go and ask Ted Blake's widow?' asked Nick. 'She is local.'

At the top of the avenue, Cain pictured the younger him all those years ago.

He stood under a tree with Nick in his shadow and looked down the pavement towards the neat house with the green door and leaded windows.

Would he and could he have actually done it? Or was it just for show to impress Harvey? Show the big detective Cain Bell was a macho as the next man.

He'd never thought about how he would hurt Ted Blake when he confronted him. Had he expected Harvey to disarm him before he had the chance to use the knife?

He had told Nick earlier they sort of fought, but they hadn't. 'Don't be a shit for brains,' Harvey had said. He had pulled the handle out of Cain's hand. Flipped the blade onto the garage roof. And banged loud enough on the front door to wake the entire neighbourhood.

Cain knocked on the green door. A mature lady in a track suit answered.

'Hi, does Ted Blake still live here? Sorry for disturbing you. I am an old friend of Ted's from the music days. He used to live in this house. I am staying in Manchester for a couple of nights with my friend Nick. Thought we'd catch a few pints with Ted. Do you have a new address for him?'

He hated playing with the emotions of an innocent caught in the crossfire. It wasn't her fault and he didn't have to punish her by recalling memories of her dead husband.

'His last known place of residence was the East Lancashire Cemetery. He died twenty years ago.'

'I am really sorry. We worked with bands together on the road before I worked in oil. Do you have any old photographs I could show my friend Nick from back in the day? Me with hair will be a laugh.'

She looked wary until Nick stepped in and said hello. 'Cain's an old mucker. You must remember me. Nick 'Boom-Boom' Forti. I live over in Unsworth. You are...'

'Dorothy. You can call me Dot.' She visibly relaxed when she recognised the name. 'You're looking well. My son is into boxing. Took after their dad although he never knew him. Ted won a few quid on you over years. I never saw any of the winnings, mind. Do you both want to come in for a coffee?'

Inside, she busied herself making coffee in the kitchen. Nick chatted away with the easy charm of a man who knew how to get into trouble with women.

Cain listened and realised for Nick chatting up women would always be a bigger problem with the booze. The chat was smooth and easy. They were getting on like a house on fire. He was making her feel important, special, without even trying. Bed would be a natural progression and another promise broken.

While they sipped coffee and dunked biscuits, Cain looked at the pictures on the wall.

There was a shrine to Ted in the corner. Framed pictures and memorabilia.

Cain studied the images. Remembered the bands. And the movies.

'I miss him so much. I never remarried. He was irreplaceable.'

'How did he die?' asked Cain.

'Cancer. Pancreatic. Quick. Less than a year from the initial diagnosis.'

'Must have been tough?'

'It was. He was a self-employed sparks. When he got ill the money dried up pretty damn quick. Friends stepped in. Helped him pay the medical bills.'

'That's kind of them.'

'We still get a Christmas card from Bob. They worked on films.'

'Bob?'

'Bob Ord. Found work for our Ted. Were you in music?'

'Music was our bread and butter.'

'He kept diaries. Said they would be his pension. Said nostalgia paid because people wanted to relive the best years of their lives. I'd like to publish them, but don't know how.'

'I have a few contacts in the book trade. Can I see them?'

'Sure.'

Dot wasn't away for long. Came downstairs with a dozen exercise books. He thanked her and opened them. Each page with large barely legible red scribble. The year was written on the front of each book. He found 1997. 'Can I hang on to them. Nick can bring them back?'

'Anytime.' She blushed when Nick smiled.

'*All Down The Line* is a great movie. When was it filmed?'

'Not sure. When Diana died. They were filming in Chanteraine and her death extended the shoot by a week. I was pregnant with Liam. Ted missed the birth.'

'When was Liam born?'

'Second of September. Ted was still in France. Flew back on the fifth. I collected him from the airport.'

'So Ted wasn't in the country the night Diana died?'

'No.'

'How come you remember the date so well?'

'Because he told me straight off he was dying. There was nothing to be done. They'd told him in France.'

Nick pushed him out the door before Cain could ask any more questions. 'We've got a party to go to Cain, say goodbye to Manchester. We don't want to be stirring up sad memories for Dot.'

Nick was right.

Any questions would be superfluous. April was right too.

There was a sense of relief that she wasn't lying to him after all.

Ted Blake couldn't have been in two places at once. April wasn't mistaken or misled. She'd been telling him the truth.

He had the proof.

He should have asked Len Harvey one more question. Any detective worth their salt should have checked if the alleged killer was actually in the country when the child was murdered. Why did he take Bob Ord's word rather than check?

There was a simple answer.

Bob Ord was the driver. Him and April had split up so soon after the birth of Summer and the death of Eric.

She could not live with the guilt that the man she loved had run over an innocent girl and driven away like the coward he was.

And all the evidence was in the secret diaries. He just needed to read them and confront Bob Ord. Would the c*** fake another epileptic fit again? Piss himself to make the con look realistic.

Would his daughter have started talking bollocks about an interventionist God?

He wasn't going to be fooled again. No wonder they wanted him out of harm's way in California.

Bob had hired his mate's son to silence April because she could not marry him with a guilty conscience.

'A penny for them?' asked Nick.

'I need to be alone for a bit.'

'You going to update me?'

'I just need time by myself,' said Cain.

Twenty-Nine.

Cain booked a room for a couple of hours in the Premier Inn at the M60 junction 17 that divided Manchester and Prestwich from Whitefield, Radcliffe and Bury.

The receptionist asked if it was for them both, she might have to check with head office.

'No, just for me. He's going to have a spot of lunch. Make sure he doesn't drink too much.'

'Are you expecting anyone else?'

Only an invisible ten-year-old ghost. Then it clicked what the sleazy receptionist really meant. People only booked by the hour if they were shagging. She thought one of them was a rent boy.

He shrugged off the implications. If it registered with Nick, he didn't seem to notice.

'What do I do while you read your exercise books? Shall I go and down a shift at the Red Manifesto. I need to be busy.'

Distracted, Cain nodded, 'Sure.'

'How do I get there? You want me to walk to Castlefield?'

Cain gave him two blue notes or was it three or four.

He wasn't looking. He wanted to read. Then he wanted to confront Bob Ord and Summer Sands.

After Nick had left the reception, Cain went into the bar of the Premier Inn and ordered a chilled bottled of Chablis.

The waitress uncorked the bottle and as a youthful jape offered him the cork to sniff.

It wasn't funny.

The place was only two steps up from Pandora's Box if it happily sold rooms by the hour.

Armed with the bottle of wine, he opened the 1997 journal.

Ted was at the heart of the whole Madchester rave scene. He worked for the Mondays and the Roses and Oasis.

When he wasn't gigging, he dabbled in film thanks to his friendship with Bob Ord.

He flicked through the journals until he reached the daily entries for *All Down The Line.*

He looked over at Little Miss Red Dress. She was playing with the coffee cups and the free biscuits. She wanted to know her killer as much as he did.

A month and a bit before Death-Day!

> *Had another bust up with Vince because he ain't pulling his weight. The bugger will get an IMDb film credit, yet I am doing his graft.*
>
> *Doing my job and his for the same pay when I am going to have another mouth to feed pretty soon. Gonna call the kid Liam after you know who. Hope he grows up as cool. Unlike Vince. Who is a lazy gobshite.*
>
> *Not fair, so I tell Bob, who tells me to man up. We all have*

to pull together. Says his own pregnant wife is busy cooking scran for the crew when she should be putting her feet up. I tell him she is top scran merchant. Could do it for a living. Says she will be busy enough feeding four mouths at home once the twins arrive.

He says Vince is keeping the crew working with pick me ups. Tells me we got to work night and day to finish the bloody movie. He can barely sleep at night .... Fortunately, Vince helps him sleep too, same as he helps me and my bloody aching back, which is too painful to endure.

Been getting worse for two years now. Dot says I should see the doctor, but what would they do? Give me a bloody aspirin.

Still, should not complain. Poncing about on a film set is far better than humping shit on and off stage every night.

Foolish me should have claimed against someone and claimed the bad back was because of a tour. The Stones could afford a payout. Bob couldn't. Trouble is I am too nice.

Was the boy already dead? Rotting inside April.

Messing with her head so she thought it was OK to have an affair with the father of the daughter killed by her epileptic husband.

At least she had the integrity to spill the beans when they were going to take oaths in front of God.

Bloody hell. Billy McGinty turns up with his heavily pregnant missus. Bob wants me to collect him and her from Nice airport. That's an hour I got to sit with the two of them in a bloody jeep.

I am trapped with a fucking lunatic who breaks legs for fun. He cut somebody with a Samurai sword in a Nippon

restaurant in George Street because he was cheeking his wife.
Crazy bastard.

I've developed a stutter. I am so nervous. I keep on farting.
Thank christ we are in an open top jeep. I don't look at
his wife at all.

She is a bit of all right even if she is up the duff. I like
my face as it is and don't want him spoiling my good looks.

Billy McGinty using a Samurai sword in the Tappenyaki
corroborated in writing. He'd been a violent psychopathic
thug for decades.

Billy is steaming annoyed. He's making me dead nervous.
He's pissed off because he has to go back early because of a
problem in Manchester that needs sorting. Only he can do it.
Bob Ord tells me I have to drive him back to Nice airport. I
tried to palm the job off on Vince, but Bob insists.

Billy can talk for England. You have to nod and agree
with everything he says in case he takes offence. Billy said all
he wanted was a few days respite from the business. A chance
to recharge the batteries. Spend a bit of quality time with Vee
and the baby boy.

He curses bloody Jimmy Cambridge. Only bloke I could
ever trust, he says. Shouldn't have taken him on a walk with
the dogs, I would have said. But I want to keep my body in
one piece, unlike poor Jimbo, so I nod in agreement and say
good deputies are hard to find.

Tell him I am struggling with Vince. He tells me not to
get on the wrong side of Vince. He's trouble looking for an
argument. He'd put a bullet in your head if he thought it
would benefit him. Why do macho men big each other up?

Billy thinks he's smarter than he actually is in the real world. He'll be lucky to survive the turn of the century before somebody takes him out.

Billy tells me to keep my nose clean and avoid the idiots. You never know when they are going to turn. I am more concerned about my back than IRA gunman and Salford drug dealers. I am going have to tests at the hospital. They sound concerned.

You never knew when they were going to go schizophrenic on you.

One word out of place and … he didn't want to know what violent men did to each other.

Cartoon violence was OK in the movies, but never in real life.

Are the stories about Billy McGinty true or merely anecdotal fantasy exaggerated with each telling?

He flicked through the film making stuff. He wanted the incriminating proof.

Back ached too much to drive. April drove us to the hospital in the jeep that Bob used for running around the lake. He wanted to use the Golf himself as he had to collect a package from Nice airport.

Shat myself most of the way. I have to remind her to drive on the right side of the road. She's a shit driver. Great cook. Don't concentrate or look at the road. Bird drivers never know left from their right.

April is dead worried about Violet, who looks like shit warmed up. She says her kid has stopped kicking her. I am praying their waters would not break on the way. Looks dead easy on the telly when they deliver bairns, but I am a lover not a midwife.

Huge sigh of relief when we reach the hospital. The two of them scoot off to the maternity unit double quick time.

I went to see Pierre La Rue, the coolest, craziest cancer consultant in the world who also plays fiddle in a cajun band.

He's going to tell me the pain in the back is a trapped nerve or poor posture and that I am a paranoid raver who has dropped too much acid.

But I am not that lucky. No Sir. Not me. This crazy Frenchman who looks like Jim Morrison from the Doors tells me I have stage 4 pancreatic cancer and I have months to live. He says if it had been spotted sooner, we might have stood a fighting chance.

Perhaps not.

It was in the lap of the Gods how much time I had left. Now. I should … damn. How do you tell people you're on a death sentence? I'll ask Bob. He knows. He always knows what to do.

Has answer for everything. Apart from dying.

Must have been before April lost the sight in her left eye although she said she lost it in her teens.

Not sure how he'd feel receiving a death sentence like that.

Ted seemed pretty philosophical. Told his wife at the airport.

Told her everything. Never mentioned the crash because it never took place.

Cain sipped the wine. It tasted shit.

Bob is euphoric and high as a kite. Cesarean birth apparently, otherwise the women and babies would be back with us.

Would have liked to see bairns. April has had a young girl. They've called her Samantha or was it Summer? Bob was pissed at the time. I like both the names.

What's the other one called? Her twin. Bob yells at me. Says there was never a twin. I must have been off my tits and been confused.

I don't argue. I don't want to spoil the good vibes.

Violet has had a boy. Named him Ryan after Giggsy.

PS: We're waiting to see the bairns but no. They're all going straight home when they leave the hospital. Thousand-mile drive. The four of them can share it.

Everyone on the set is a bit disappointed. Still, you know what women are like … think I'd be the same if someone cut my stomach open and took out a huge growth from inside me.

That's what I thought they'd do with the pancreatic cancer. Cut it out. But they said it was too late.

Was there a twin or was it lies?

Ted was an unreliable witness with his ramblings and prodigious drug intake and a pending death sentence of his own.

Maybe he was confused. Maybe he was telling the truth.

The same logic could be applied to Bob Ord too. No mention of anyone called Eric.

We're all packed up and about to split from our home for

the last three months. I am missing Dot and baby Liam.

Cannot wait to see them. Terrified at the same time.

Ready to go home. Say goodbye to the bluest lake ever. I'll never return unless the man upstairs wants to break his rules and intervene. He didn't do no favours for the queen of hearts so why should he make an exception for a Bury rat boy?

Don't answer. To be honest, I'll be glad to go home.

Since April left, the scran has been crap. Vince might score top drugs, but he ain't no saint in the kitchen.

No other mug is volunteering to cook. It's all gone a bit shit since Bob left. Him and Billy are big buddies, much bigger than I thought.

Fucking insane.

Last entry.

The death of the Queen of Hearts, killed a couple of days ago in Paris in a drunken car crash, has gutted the remaining crew who are packing up.

Never drink drive, it's a fool's game. Or when you're tired.

Vince has elected himself as the self-proclaimed leader of the gang and nobody wants to argue with him.

I am all for a peaceful life, so I try to be his mate and make conversation. I said I hoped Bob, Billy, April, Violet and kids weren't involved and he said they were already back home. I said I hope we get paid because methinks Bob's probably over budget.

Vince said why did he think Billy was here. For the suntan? He said Bob's a fool if he's borrowed from Billy M. He's going to be paying top dollar interest.

Not that Vince cares. As long as he gets paid, he doesn't

care what he has to do. Tells me he likes the movie lark. Can I get him another movie or work with a band? I almost tell him my news, except I don't trust him. I've not told a soul yet apart from Bob. My family has to be told face to face. I told Bob I am going to be dead skint if I don't work. He makes a joke about having to find a new electrician. I tell him Vince is fully up for it. He's too distracted to get my sarcasm.

Before he leaves, we tell each we'll meet up soon enough to wet Summer's head back in Manchester.

Hopefully we'd do it before I kick the bucket.

You know, I'll be in bloody heaven after spending my time in hell. That's the sort of thing Keef would say.

My legacy will be this little diary. Wonder if anyone will ever read it?

Tara for now.

See you around.

Ted Blake was not the driver.

He had definitive proof.

But Bob Ord could have been.

Little Miss Red Dress was sat on the loo seat.

She smiled. 'Thank you Daddy, what you are you going to do to the man who killed me?'

Thirty.

The man who had killed his daughter was living it large in his apartment five miles down the Bury New Road.

He had destroyed his old life in Manchester, and he was offering him a new one in California.

With the Blake journals under his arm, Cain slunk out the Premier Inn like an anxious geography teacher anticipating a mind-numbing weekend of marking.

The roar of racing cars or speeding HGVs on the nearby motorway made him jump.

Was this how suicides felt before they leapt into the void, swallowed handfuls of tablets or stepped in front of the InterCity Express linking Manchester, London and certain demise?

Devoid of feeling, wiped out emotionally, he knew everything, and nothing had changed.

His life and options were so much easier when Ted Blake had been the driver that ploughed into Little Miss Red Dress.

Ted was dead and you could not punch a man's ashes.

Now he had to make decisions when he'd rather drink Chablis and nosh on fresh pan-fried scallops cooked with garlic, ginger and a hint of soy sauce, his and April's favourite Sunday morning pick-me-up.

What to do?

He was Hamlet, the king of procrastination knowing something, many things, were rotten in Rainy City, but he was frozen into inaction. His concocted proof was not enough.

He needed more.

He called Rachel Roberts and went straight through to voicemail. He left a message. 'You've got your cash. Now give me the tapes. I know April's story anyway about the dead baby and the real driver who killed my daughter. So let's stop pissing about before anyone else gets hurt.'

He thought about redoing the message with less inflammatory words.

'Piss, shit and fuck,' he said at the missed opportunity.

Three women gave him an extra wide berth. They probably thought he was on day release from the mental health unit hidden behind Tescos and TGI Fridays.

He'd already forgotten them when a black Range Rover pulled alongside him and slowed down.

Was this the end?

The window on the passenger side was wound down slowly, revealing … an empty seat.

Vince Crane behind the wheel. 'Climb on board. Nick said you might need a friend to lean on.'

Could he trust Vince? Was he Billy McGinty's man? Only one way to find out.

'Thanks.' Cain clicked on the seatbelt and sat back in

the leather seat of the four-wheel drive, the pile of exercise books on his lap.

'What you got there?'

'Diaries of a Rock'n'Roll Roadie.'

'Really?'

'Bloke called Ted Blake. Do you know him?'

'Nothing springs to mind,' said Vince, 'then again I am shite with names. A face I never forget but names…'

'You're in the book. You and Ted worked on *All Down The Line*.'

'Did we? If you can remember the nineties, you weren't there,' said Vince. 'Ted Blake, was he a freelance sparks?'

Cain admired his speed of thought. 'You offering me more advice about messing with Billy McGinty?'

'Last thing on my mind. I am on your side. Always have been. Do you want to share your thoughts?'

'About?'

'Everything. Little birdies tell me you're leaving on a jet plane with April. Is it true?' asked Vince. 'California?'

'I am thinking about it.'

'Can I buy the Red Manifesto off you?'

'You don't know the first thing about running a restaurant.'

'Neither do you,' grinned Vince.

'You couldn't afford it? Even with your extortionate wages. You make more than April and me combined.'

'Lot of palms to grease. Besides, I am sure we can work out a good deal … cash and goods or services in kind.'

'What does that mean?'

'Whatever you want it to … give me a yes about the cash and then we'll get serious.'

'Perhaps you should call a spade a spade.'

'You play the middle-class prick with aplomb, but you're not dumb with it.'

'Can you drop me at the hospital?'

'I was taking you to the Manifesto. Sign and seal a deal over a bottle of Chablis, I am paying.'

'I need to speak to April.'

Crane made an ostentatious u-turn at the Hilton/Scholes Lane crossroads without giving a damn about an angry motorists flashing him. 'If I stopped and got out the fucker would crap himself empty before my left foot had touched the ground.'

'If you say it's Christmas, most people would agree with you even in the middle of July.'

'You're right there, Boss. Let me elaborate. Services in kind is exactly that. You've got a few problems. I can make them go away. They won't be the first people I've executed. You get revenge for April and for Hannah.'

'What do you mean?'

'Strike a deal and I'll tell you everything.'

Cain stared hard at his friend and head of security who was already eyeballing women walking around the outskirts of Heaton Park and marking them out of ten under his breath.

He would hand him the keys straight away except the inner journalist stopped him: you always needed two sources to verify anything before you could print! The proof was in the exercise books.

In the hospital, he put Vince in a box. Slammed the lid shut. He could open it again later.

April looked at peace with the world. The urgency

surrounding her immediate treatment had been downgraded.

They had given her a private room on the high dependency unit next door to ICU. It had taken five minutes to establish that when he had arrived.

He asked if she had had any visitors and was told she hadn't.

Nobody seemed concerned about his presence, so he simply went into her room sat down beside the most beautiful woman in the world.

Little Miss Red Dress was sat on the other side of the room. Picked up a magazine. Started flicking through the pages. 'Can you hear me? Are you still with us? Squeeze my hand if you can hear me?'

There was no reaction. Not that he expected one. Her hand felt warmer than it had in ICU. Raj Ghandi had explained they lowered her temperature to reduce the swelling.

'Daddy, she's like me,' said Little Miss Red Dress, looking up from her glossy magazine.

'Not officially. There is still hope. That's why we're all going to the USA soon.'

'Can I come?' asked Little Miss Red Dress. 'I'll be happier there.'

'Wherever I go, you go,' said Cain. He could not bring himself to say you don't exist anymore in a physical form. You're just my imagination running with me, again and again and again. Mick and Keef and the boys had covered the Temptations soul classic in typical Stones fashion. They were on the verge of karaoke by the time they were releasing *Some Girls*. But when they recorded *Exile,* they were as dangerous as Billy McGinty. Bob Ord had tapped into that danger.

Used it to big up *Madchester*. Smart dude. Shit driver.

He held April's hand. 'I wish you'd told me. Trusted me about Eric. We would have shared the grief city blues.' He glanced over at Little Miss Red Dress deep in her magazine. 'We're going on a trip soon. They say it will make you better, but I don't know. You know the USA. You never know what is fake and real when it comes to making money. '

Her noticed her medical notes had been left on the trolley at the end of the bed.

Like any good reporter he felt the urge to have a peek at what they were really saying about April.

What was the cold reality compared to the soft soap they used to keep relatives on side?

He picked them up and flicked through them although he might as well have been reading Japanese menu.

The medical language was Double Dutch, random complicated words he would struggle to pronounce without help from a doctor or a nurse, a bit like commentators running through multi-national Premiership teams.

He wondered why his mind was wired to wander at times of stress? Black comedy and banter masked your emotions and were cheaper and less damaging than alcohol and coke.

He checked out the dates on the medical records. They went back several decades into the dark ages of the last century when she had lost the sight in one eye and a child was stillborn.

Nothing jumped out at him. No wording was obvious. In 1997, she'd given birth to two healthy twins in France. No mention of a Caesarean section. In 2004, she'd had a hysterectomy. Did that operation explain the scarring on her abdomen and the Caesarean was another secret lie?

Thirty-One.

Confused by his inability to understand the medical jargon, he did what all good journalists did: asked somebody in authority who happened to be manning the front desk of the high dependency unit.

'Hello Barbara,' said Cain, looking at the name badge of the ward Sister Barbara Jackson sat down at the work station. 'There is a problem with April Sands' notes. I cannot see any mention of her losing the sight in one eye. Nothing optical jumps out of me. I was under the impression she had a stillborn child in 1997. Again, there is no mention.'

'Not sure I can do that. Who are you?' she asked.

'Cain Bell, April's fiancée.'

'One of the consultants wants to speak to you. Said it is very important. Can you wait for me while I contact him?'

Cain glanced at the clock above the Gothic Sister's head. 'Time is against me. I've got a plane to catch in a bit if you answer my questions and cross reference them on screen.'

She took the notes and skim read them quickly. She would rather Cain stayed than left her to explain to an exasperated consultant why he had gone. 'There's no mention of any problems with her eyes and both babies were born healthy.'

'Could the medical records be wrong? Mistakes can happen. Important things are missed off, especially from a long time ago or when the twins were born in a foreign country.'

'Says here the kids were home births in Salford,' she smiled. 'Only a foreign country to some.'

Raj Ghandi arrived six minutes later dressed in civilian clothing. They exchanged pleasantries. He explained he had been lecturing medical students but was keen to have an off-the-record word with him in private.

'How is she doing?' asked Cain.

'No apologies for my bluntness. I would be doing April and yourself a disservice if I avoided stating the obvious.'

'I appreciate your honesty.'

'Maybe you won't be so appreciative after I've finished.'

'I am a former journalist. I am used to bad news,' said Cain.

'April's not going to recover. Full stop. There are no changes in her condition. The care team looking after her is unanimous. Your next of kin want to fly her to California. A heavy-duty legal letter that scared the shit out of this hospital trust. I am not so easy to intimidate.'

'I am sorry, It is nothing to do with me.'

'She's not going to get better. She is brain dead.'

'Have you spoken to her family?'

'I am not allowed to according to the letter. But you're not on the list, so I am speaking to you man to man.'

Cain couldn't fault Raj's passion. He was a taking a huge risk having this conversation. If Cain took it the wrong way, he could be surfing in the deep thick stuff. 'Will I start to see her like Little Miss Red Dress?'

'Pardon.'

This was not the time for Cain to explain about visions of dead loved ones.

He was surprised he wasn't more shocked by the news from the surgeon.

Perhaps he had expected it all along. He was born unlucky. 'What do you want me to do?'

'Speak to the next of kin. Try and make them see sense. Use your powers of persuasion to stop wasting everyone's time. She deserves to rest in peace.'

'I'll give a good shot,' said Cain.

He shook the pudgy hand of the senior consultant. Held the grip to show he appreciated all he had done for the woman who had once been the most beautiful in the world. Now, he wasn't sure whether she deserved that status.

'I've got one question for you?'

'Fire away.'

'What are the chances you're wrong? Could you be mistaken? You read about it all the time. People coming out of comas years later.'

'No.'

'Definitely. You'd bet your own life?'

'I don't gamble. I deal with evidence. And that is definitive. I am sorry.'

'No need. You did all you could.' After Raj had gone Cain sat down with April and Little Miss Red Dress.

Lying is a big call. We all do it every day don't we? Little White Lies to make sure we don't offend someone by being unnecessarily cruel. But the Big Black Lies, the dark ones that are underpinned by sinister motives, they are less easy to forgive.

Did you know who I was back in that restaurant?

Did you love me out of pity and guilt?

Did you know all along that your husband had killed her Hannah?

Was that what drove you away from your own child to live a nomadic lifestyle free from emotion.

Is that it?

Is Rachel Roberts' twelve grand to keep a secret?

Or is it about a stillborn child? That wasn't your fault. Not your shame. Shit happens. Not that I am sure why. Why did they attack you? What line did you cross? You were going to tell me it was Bob Ord, your husband, who is best mates with Billy McGinty. Perhaps he was driving the car and not the film producer.

I'll never know because you can never tell me, but Bob can and it is time he told me the truth.

He looked over at Little Miss Red Dress, who stared at him intently.

'What about revenge?'

'What about it?'

'An eye for an eye, Daddy. An eye for an eye.'

She wouldn't have said it. No way. She was ten when she passed away. A tall skinny child who believed only what me and her mum had shown and told her.

She hadn't lived long enough to have her dreams dashed and her imagination placed in cold storage. The cynicism bug had yet to infect her. She would never age. Like Monroe and Diane never age and wither. Forever young. Like Hannah.

I was putting words into her mouth that should have come from mine.

What did I want?

As Nick had asked, how did my justice taste, look and smell?

Simple, really. I wanted the truth. And then what? Public shaming, humiliation, a day of reckoning and a hastily rewritten obituary for a famous hit and run film financier who killed a ten-year-old child and never admitted what he had done?

Bob Ord's Wikipedia page would need to be edited. Like yours, April. Would a ruined reputation be punishment enough for a man who wanted to protect his good name at all costs? Bob Ord was relatively easy. Ryan McGinty, and whoever sent him, was more difficult. They didn't have a stake in society beyond what they could steal, hurt or hinder.

I am talking crap. Distracting myself. You're dead, April, unofficially, you've passed onto the other side.

You're gone for good and I'll only ever see you in my imagination, but you're not pure and untainted, like Hannah was.

There is so much you hid from me that you're almost a stranger and everything we did together as a couple is suspect.

Is that how I am going to feel whenever I think about you?

The most beautiful and most flawed woman in the world?

Don't worry. I don't expect an answer. There are none. And what does it matter?

Tomorrow I leave for California and continue to play out a Big Black Lie for the rest of my life.

Once Hal gets me a green card, the world is my oyster.

You know, I'll go silently, without any fuss or a fanfare, or any long, drawn out goodbyes.

My survival matters more than revenge and justice.

They are just words. You know one thing this has taught me? Words are pointless. They have no value or currency. They have no meaning beyond sounding good if your voice and acting skills grabbed the listener's attention. What did any words matter if what was said one minute could be forgotten the next?

Cain stood up. Little Miss Red Dress had vacated her space. Time to man up. Be sensible and look after number one. It's what anyone in his position would do.

Thirty-Two.

The walk of shame started the second Cain heard the door slowly bang behind him as he left April's room.

He waved goodbye to Gothic Barbara at the central desk. She was busy messing with the computer and the phone.

Perhaps she was talking to the Americans about transporting his dead fiancée five thousand miles west to California.

A total waste of time, according to Raj, who had no reason to lie to him.

Cain speed walked from the hospital. Took him ten minutes to connect with the Bury Old Road and Cheetham Hill.

By the time he was half-way to Manchester's Northern Quarter, he'd swallowed a pragmatism pill: he was leaving, he needed extra cash for a float to tide him over his brand new beginnings.

He called Rachel Roberts. Went straight to voicemail again. Left her another message. 'Disappointed you've not come back to me. Not interested in your deal anymore. I want my twelve grand back today. I'll send someone to get it. Pay me back or you'll be sorry.'

Next he called Vince Crane. Went to voicemail as well. Unusual for the Irishman not to answer. 'I've got a few errands to run, but you're on for the restaurant if you still want to invest, at least my share of it. A chunk of cash upfront, and we'll talk about the rest of the deal if you're free tomorrow 9am at the Manifesto.'

He cut the call. Then realised he could save a bit of time and energy if Vince did him a favour. He rang back. Left another message. 'Can you pop over to Rachel Roberts' place. Her address is on the EPOS system. She's had twelve grand of my money in fifities and I want it back. Bring it with you at 9am. Ask Nick to give me a call too.'

Summer was next up.

She answered within two rings. He asked her what time they were flying tomorrow? She told him they had to be at the airport two hours before take-off. If he needed any help packing, just shout. She was travelling light with Bob's American Express card in her back pocket. She would buy new. Cain thought she sounded remarkably cheerful for a daughter in mourning. 'Is Nick there?' he asked.

'With his wife, apparently. They've reconciled. He called and left a message. When are you back?'

'I've got to tie up a few loose ends before we travel,' he said, pleased for Nick. At least some good had come out of the whole debacle.

He stopped to catch his breath. Sat on a wall and watched commerce in action. Busy people flogging fast fashion, jewellery and mobile phones. He thought about calling Violet. Advising her boy to run off to Spain and hide out in

Costa Del Crime. His Nazi tattoo would be right at home in that fascist enclave. That would give him a few seconds satisfaction.

What did revenge look like?

Public humiliation? He called Matt Stark, who answered faster than Summer.

'Been waiting for you to get in touch. Thought it best to give you space. Then I hear on the grapevine you're taking her to America. Is it true?'

'Yes.'

'You could have told me. When are you going?'

'Tomorrow.'

'Christ, alive. What's the rush? Is she OK to travel?'

Valid questions from a proper professional reporter who got to the point without any flannel.

But April wasn't the story. She was yesterday's papers. The story was bigger than her.

And he was about to hand it on a plate to his mate. 'I leave April's health to the professionals. I know who killed your niece, my daughter.'

'You been drinking?'

'Bob Ord. April's ex.'

'He was driving?'

'Yes.'

'Any evidence?'

'Better than that. He's going to give you a world exclusive.'

'He is?'

'Your lucky day. We go halves on syndication. Agreed?'

'Fine. Has he confessed?'

'Not yet, but he will and then we'll set up the story. Sit on it until I call you tomorrow morning. Tell no one.'

'Cain?'

'Laters.'

One down. The law could deal with the next bottle to fall off the green wall. He dialled Rita Rock. Seven rings before she picked up. 'I want to make a statement. Identify April's attackers.'

'I am off duty, Cain. About to get ready for a party. I am in tomorrow.'

'Now or never, Rita. I am flying out to California in less than 24 hours.'

'Holiday?'

'Fresh start.'

'Give me five minutes.'

Two hours later Rita Rock turned off the video camera and collated the paperwork for Cain to sign.

She was dressed in jeans and black jumper, hair pulled away from a face free of make-up.

She looked even more weary without the slap. If she was miffed because her day had been interrupted, she hid her disappointment well.

She remained professional and courteous throughout, but there was an edge.

She had brought a young black colleague in called Stephanie to help her with the admin and the filming.

Steph did the small talk while Rita filmed, asked the questions and recorded his statement. 'Are we finished?'

'Just sign here.'

So, he did. Wrote out his signature big and clear to reflect the size of his personality and depth of his courage. 'When are you going to arrest them?'

'Not up to me. I am just a cog in a very big slow turning

wheel. But I do appreciate your witness statement. We can reach you on this number and email?'

'Yes.'

'Do you want a lift anywhere.'

'Walking is good,' he said and sauntered slowly from the GMP head office back towards the city centre.

His home towered over the north end of the city. New gigantic builds as tall and intimidating were under construction.

Manchester would be a global hub rather than European. He would resign his job from a beach in California with the sun on his back.

He had hated being PAYE for the majority of his life, jumping to the tune of others.

He walked into Atlas, a six-iron golf shot from home. Ordered a bottle of Chablis.

Put it on the Red Manifesto card.

Vince would pick up the tab when the monthly bill came through.

He was done.

Hadn't taken long at all.

One more conversation and a confession. Then he could kiss goodbye to Rainy City with a clear conscience.

Thirty-Three.

He was sat by himself in the corner. Felt hungry. Flicked through the menu.

Red Manifesto's was far better, but he didn't want to see the place again. The building and the brand was synonymous with April, unless they rebranded. But he didn't have the will, the authority or the cash.

He looked at the battery on the iPhone. It was nearly as exhausted as he was.

Had enough energy for one more call. He asked Summer to come alone to Atlas. He needed a word in private.

Ten minutes later he showed her the menu in case she wanted to eat.

He wondered if they would be able to eat while discussing switching off machines and letting a woman you loved die.

Only Summer had the power to cut the electricity. 'I've been to the hospital today.'

'I went too. First thing,' said Summer. 'You'd never think she was ill looking at her.'

'Did anyone speak to you about her condition.'

'No. The old man was with a couple of medical experts from the insurance company. I left them to it.'

'I spoke to Raj this afternoon. He said your mother was clinically dead.' He tried to keep his voice calm and authoritative. Medical staff broke bad news all the time.

'He's lying. He doesn't know for sure. Nobody knows how God works.'

Cain sipped his wine. Waited as a waitress delivered a food platter.

He looked around for Little Miss Red Dress. She wasn't there. He'd given her the night off. Perhaps she was already in California with April. The thought pleased him. 'There's no easy, nice way to say this. You are the next of kin and it is your responsibility to take an awful decision. If I thought there was even the slimmest of chances, I'd be batting with you. But they've done the head scans. There is no activity. No life.'

'What if I say no?'

'We carry on with the charade. We carry on pretending. And we lie to each other that she will get better. Each day, we die a little too.'

'Do you mean that or does it just sound good? My mum called you her Guitar Hero because you made her happy and now you want to kill her?' The food was untouched. She sipped the glass of wine. Tears rolled unrestrained down her face. He wanted to cry too, but resisted. He had to lead by example. 'Give me five minutes. I need a cigarette.'

The waitress asked her if everything was all right as she left.

They both glanced over at him. The waitress probably assumed it was a relationship ending. An older sugar daddy telling a young innocent the party was over. Everyone made assumptions. Jumped to conclusions without any evidence, beyond what they wanted to see on social media.

Outside she rolled a cigarette. The wind didn't stop her lighting up. Was she saying a prayer for her mother? Asking for God's advice? She was just a kid about to lose her mother and have her father exposed as a hit-and-run murderer. Hannah would have been thirty. She might have been working in a bar like the waitress who had checked Summer's welfare. That would have made him proud, if Hannah put others first.

April would have done the same. Or would she? He'd never know. Their bond had proved to be skin deep.

Summer was back in the bar. Sat herself down. 'Can I sleep on it?' she asked. 'It's too big a decision to take by myself. I need to speak to my dad.'

'So do I,' he said. 'I've got a MacBook at the Red Manifesto. Would you collect it for me? Give me an hour to chat with Bob.'

'About?'

'My own daughter.'

'Be careful, don't stress him out. I am worried he might have a stroke.'

Bob didn't look too stressed when Cain walked into the flat and let the door close.

The old man was lying on the sofa watching Netflix and eating peanuts. 'Make us a cup of tea, love. What did that lanky streak of piss want? Has he changed his mind about America, the ungrateful knob?'

'Make your own,' said Cain. 'Sit up.' He walked into the sitting room and glanced out at the panoramic view.

Tomorrow he'd be looking at beach with blue seas and golden sands and girls with straight white teeth and washboard stomachs.

'I was only having a laugh, mate, wind your neck in.'

'I won't play games with you so I'll get to the point. You drove the car that killed my daughter on 31st August 1997.'

'Did I?' responded Bob. The shock of the allegation straightened him up. 'You are a prick. A real knob. April doesn't know how lucky she is.'

Cain ignored the insults. This was how he expected a coward like Bob Ord to react. When he heard the evidence and the proposition, he would change his tune. 'I listened to your story without interruption. Now you need to show me the same courtesy. That's sounds like a reasonable request?'

'If you must, but you were wasting your time. It wasn't me.'

'Because you're epileptic? A convenient excuse?'

'Check my medical records, nobby.'

> *My daughter was hit by a speeding car with false number plates on Bury New Road in Prestwich.*
>
> *The impact tossed her in the air and broke her neck.*
>
> *The car that hit her slowed down.*
>
> *Almost stopped.*
>
> *Then sped off again.*
>
> *I was there. I saw it all. The driver had the opportunity to stop but decided to run.*
>
> *I held my daughter's broken body in my arms.*
>
> *Her head moved unnaturally because of the break in her neck.*
>
> *The police found what they assumed was the vehicle*

burned out in Salford Quays in the early hours of the morning.

Whoever destroyed the car, did an impressive job. There was no DNA and forensics on the car according to the detective heading the investigation and the CCTV footage was inclusive, the resolution not high enough to capture who was driving.

You had known the investigating detective well enough to invite him for a busman's holiday on the set of All Down The Line.

You returned the favour back in England. Grassed up the driver of the car that killed my daughter.

Drum roll. Ted Blake took the blame for you.

Once the investigation stopped, you knew no-one would be tapping you on the shoulder.

You knew the father would not rest until he had closure. Your plan would have worked except ....

'Absolute bollocks.'
'Let me finish.'

...You knew Ted had terminal pancreatic cancer. Had months left. You persuaded Ted to 'confess' to Len Harvey he was the one. Len told me and I was satisfied because why would a dying man lie?

Fast forward two decades and when I propose to your ex-wife, she tells me Ted Blake did not drive the car. She was attacked before she fully explains what she meant.

Only me, Ted and Len knew about the secret confession ... plus the people scapegoated him. You directly and April indirectly. I did my own checking. Ted Blake was still in

France when Hannah was killed. His journals confirm he was still in France until early September.

'Is that it? I've never driven a car because of my epilepsy.'

'Would that be your excuse in a court? Perhaps you could say you had a fit at the wheel and lost control of the lethal weapon. Hit a young girl by mistake. I've seen you fit. You're really groggy in the immediate aftermath. Like you've undergone electric shock treatment. Your brains have been scrambled. You recovered quickly enough to drive away. A very speedy recovery. Might not wash with a jury. The epilepsy card is not a good excuse.'

'You're a very creative thinker. A talented storyteller. Hollywood needs men with fertile imaginations. You might do better with Hal if you pitch your wild stories to him rather than writing bloody press releases nobody ever reads. Why are you bothering with this all those years after the event?'

'Confess. You'll feel far better about yourself,' said Cain.

'You're not listening to me. Deaf as well as dumb. You're getting on my tits.' Bob picked up the mobile by his left hip and pressed the screen a couple times.

Seconds later, Cain's mobile rang. He didn't recognise the number but answered on the first ring.

'Hello?'

'I am outside.'

'Who is this?'

'Billy McGinty.'

'I am busy. Call me tomorrow.'

'Time for a chat. Either you come out or I'll come in. You decide how much of a scene you want to create.'

Thirty-Four.

At last. The time had come. The waiting was over. No more excuses. He was going to meet the man who pulled strings. Broke the bones. And determined who lived and who died.

Bob Ord shook his head ruefully. 'Sorry, you left me no choice. Not involved him by harassing me. Too dumb to listen.'

Cain noticed Ord's demeanour had changed.

Did the film financier know what was coming? Did he know about the dogs and swallowing Samurai swords?

There was only way to find out. Face Billy down. Should he get a weapon? Find a knife?

He could ask Little Miss Red Dress to accompany him, but a figment of his imagination was hardly going to help him. 'Just tell your story to the media. We don't have to tell the police. There are probably time limits on road traffic accidents.'

'Wonder if it is too late to refund your plane ticket?' asked Ord. 'Where's Summer?'

'Getting my laptop from the Manifesto.'

There was loud knock on the door. Was it her?

Of course not. She had a key.

'You could call the police,' said Bob. 'They might be able to save you, if they get here within the next two or three minutes.'

Was Ord laughing at him? No time to decide. He had to focus on McGinty.

He left his phone on the dining room table. Took the apartment keys off his key ring. He wasn't going to gift them the car in the garage downstairs or give them free access to the Red Manifesto.

He started to move towards the front door. Stopped for a beat or two. Thinking on his feet, he could always call Vince. Ask him to mediate. Stop them doing what they were going to do. Simply swivel and walk back to the mobile.

There was another loud impatient knock. He was about to be reunited with April sooner than he anticipated. 'Here I come, April,' he said, under his breath. 'Time to put the grease in the frying pan.'

Cain opened the door. Two Scars stood there with another man dressed the same as him in all black.

'Follow me.'

Cain expected them to go down, but they went up through a service door marked strictly private. They were in the maintenance section of the building. They went through four more doors. Then the two men stopped. Ushered Cain forward. He was hit by a strong gust of wind. He was on the roof of the one the tallest residential buildings in the UK.

Heard the door shut behind him.

From behind the shadows of the blades came the big bossman dressed in a loud colourful shirt and white chinos.

Had a slight pot belly and, despite the dusky twilight, an orange tan that contrasted with the super white crowns in his mouth.

Cain wondered momentarily how a man who looked like a geeky uncle on holiday in Benidorm could rule the city's underworld.

'Wow. This your first time up here?'

'Yes,' said Cain.

'Me too. Always wanted to come up and have a look. Never had a good enough reason, until now.' Billy McGinty motioned for Cain to come closer. 'Mind you don't trip. A long way to fall and there's no safety net.'

'OK.' Cain did as he was told. Gingerly made his way forwards. Each step was a test of his nerve. Don't look down. Don't think about how high you are. Don't show him you're scared shitless.

'Come closer because it hard to talk. In really bad weather this skyscraper whistles. Cost £150m to build and they made a fundamental mistake. Three times they've tried to fix it. Three times they've failed. This glass blade facade has caused so much trouble for the owners that I bet they wish they'd never built it. Except for that Simpson architect dude. He's sitting pretty beneath us. Too much trouble for everyone else. Just like you're causing me lots of trouble when you should be flying off to the USA where you can do some good helping my good friend April Sands get better.'

'You started it,' said Cain. 'This is all down to you and your son!'

'Did I?' asked Billy. 'You've been giving false statements to Rita Rock about my boy and my brother-in-law attacking your fiancée when everyone knows it was n*****s that attacked you. You've been talking shit to your mate Matty about an exclusive story, falsely claiming my mate Bob Ord killed your child in a car accident in bloody Prestwich twenty years ago.'

'Was that *n******s too?'

'Crazy motherfucker, give you that. You not seen what I did to Two Smiles? Cut his face wide open with a Samurai sword because he talked too loudly about matters that were strictly confidential.'

'Were you there too? Let my girl die. Knock down a ten-year-old and race off? That you?' Cain was amazed his voice sounded so calm, like he was delivering a script on a stage.

Billy McGinty slow hand clapped. Stepped closer to Cain. Half a foot smaller. 'We are entering the corridor of uncertainty. You think you are smarter than me because you're good with words, but you're buying into conspiracy theories and inventing your own.'

'Which bit isn't true? Ted Blake was a patsy hired by Bob Ord to take the blame for his bad driving. Blake wasn't even in the country when my baby's neck was snapped in two.'

'You've got it all wrong. Come with me and I'll explain perception to you.'

'Where we going?'

Before Cain could refuse, he felt the smaller man put his arm around his shoulders and pull him towards skyscraper's edge. This was it. The long short goodbye. Should he resist now or nearer? There was a metal rail but the barrier was a bit low for his high centre of gravity.

'Before I came to see you tonight, they found a body. Between your restaurant and Deansgate Locks. Walking over to this place, I had little look around. I am a naturally inquisitive man.' Billy pointed to Bridge 101 and the canal path where blue lights were flashing.

Cain could see paramedics trying to revive somebody dressed in pink. 'Poor bloke.'

'A woman actually. I recognised her. Rachel Roberts. No one knows her name yet. Will take dibble at least 24 hours to ID her formally. You'll be at the airport. Preparing to live the good life in California. They won't check Rachel's phone and all her messages immediately. Take them another two or three days to start doing that, longer if they think she is a junky suicide. But if they think it is murder ...'

'What are trying to tell me?'

'Perception. Two Smiles could call dim dibble. Tell them you and Rachael Roberts were doing business before she kicked the bucket. Say you were buying tapes that would incriminate your coma girl fiancée in serious crimes. I reckon those words to the right guys would get you a month on remand. No lawyer will touch you because I'll put the word out. With my contacts, I must be able to find the two that attacked you. They've probably fucked off back to Pakistan or the Caribbean, but they'll be all too happy to say they were drug mules for you, April and Vince Crane. Not just dealing class A in your poxy restaurant but importing too. That is a whole new set of offences. As an honest citizen, it is my duty to talk to the police if we suspect a crime is taking place.'

'Everyone else knows you're a grass,' said Cain. If he was going to fall from the sky, he was going to go down talking.

'You're a very funny man.' Billy grinned at Cain. Tweaked his ear hard. Had the bastard pulled it off or used a knife on him? 'You're an educated man, you did a history degree?'

Cain nodded. 'While you were robbing lead from Salford churches, I was writing essays.'

'Another view is Rachel Roberts decided blackmail was a good earner. Upset the wrong people and is nothing to do with you or April. Truth is, I don't know why Rachel Roberts died tonight. But I am not pretending to be Columbo with outsized clown feet. Vince Crane told you. Two Smiles told you. Violet told you. And now I am telling you. N*****s attacked April and if Len Harvey said Ted Blake was the driver, then why do you want to disbelieve him?'

'What are you going to do? Kill me? Throw me over the edge? Make it look like a depressed man topping himself?'

'You ever thought of doing stand-up? Girls like a man with a sense of humour. Some men think it is a big knob. We know better. If you make a girl laugh, you can make her come too.'

'All I want is the truth about Hannah and April. That's all,' said Cain. 'Do you want me to get on my knees and beg?'

'And what would you do with the information?' asked Billy.

'I've already done it.'

'You were bragging about that earlier. Rita Rock? Our lawyers are better than their lawyers and I can scare you more than you scare me.'

'That's where you're wrong. I have already won. Beaten you, hands down. Standing up to you here. You cannot hurt me anymore. Dying would be a relief. But if you push me over, we'll see if the two of us can fly together,' said Cain.

What did Nick say? Everyone had a plan until they were punched in the mouth.

His free left hand went around the head of Billy. He pulled his head close into his chest. Hit him with three blows.

Cain sank to the ground. His size and extra weight brought down the gangster with him. Teeth bit into the side of his hand. He pounded the head until the teeth let go. 'Who killed my daughter?'

'Let go.'

Cain shifted towards the edge. Could he flip them both over? 'Why did your son attack my fiancée?'

Hands were pulling at his arms to break the bear hug. His face was slapped furiously as a voice hissed for him to let go, let go, let go, let go.

He lay on the ground spread-eagled and exhausted. His chest heaved as he tried to catch his breath. Draw oxygen into his lungs.

He was dead.

He grinned hugely at the heavens. Knew Nick Forti would have been proud the way he fought.

He was dead and he'd soon by joining Hannah and April eating the best food and listening to the greatest rock and roll names that ever lived and died…. Jimi Hendrix, Duane and Dicky, Ronnie Van Zant and the rest of the good old Skynyrd rednecks, Bob Marley and John Lennon, Gram Parsons and Brian Jones, Keith Moon, Lou Reed, Kurt Cobain, Buddy Holly, Marvin Gaye, Janis Joplin, Ian Curtis, Johnny Cash, Townes, Ronson and Bowie, Joe and Sid, Buff and Pete …

Forget Sonny's comment that someday they'll write a blues song with a slow guitar, soft trump and a bell for fighters. That lot would make a right racket.

Thirty-Five.

Cain was surprisingly fit for his age and size. Coastal walks at weekends, squash and tennis during the week and a healthy diet had repaired much of the damage of the hedonism years.

He could feel his heart rate slow and return to normal within a minute. His left hand throbbed as if somebody had tried to bite a huge chunk out of him. They had and it hurt like hell.

When he sat up, they would toy with him like a weird kid pulling off the legs of a spider or tearing the wings of butterfly.

They could mock him as much as they wanted but he had won. He had stood up to them. He had gone down fighting. Like the falling man from the twin towers, he had embraced his own death. He would not fall to earth. Rather he would fly. He would not panic as gravity pulled him down. He would appear relaxed. Float through the air with the greatest of ease. He would not die an ugly death, but he would free himself finally from the shackles of shallow human existence.

Like a diver from the highest board at the Olympics, Cain would try to remain perfectly vertical all down the lines of the glass building behind him.

If somebody happened to capture his fall to earth in the night sky, he would go viral, an image that would be seen by billions, a final act that could never be ignored or forgotten.

The establishment would have to find the truth about his fall from grace.

He raised his body in one movement. Surprised he still had the capacity to move without any real effort.

He expected the gangsters to throw him from the top of *Beaten Towers*. He grinned at the pun. Should be called *Victory Towers*.

He should have done stand-up.

There was nobody there.

He looked around.

The roof was empty.

Just him and a sore hand with teeth marks and a lot of blood.

They will have locked him on the roof. He would freeze overnight. Hypothermia would do for him.

He picked himself up and gingerly made his way slowly toward the roof opening. Carefully he climbed down the ladder, waiting to be jumped as he descended.

He entered his apartment. Again, nothing. No TV, no sound. He checked each of the rooms. They were all empty.

He had expected to see Bob Ord slumped in front of his giant TV screen, but he'd gone. No sign of Summer or his MacBook.

He looked out of the window to where Rachel Roberts had been fished from the canal, if it had been her. Why would you trust the word of a gangster when he could kill and maim with impunity? There was only one blue light vehicle left at the scene.

He inspected his wound in the en suite bathroom. Washed it under the cold-water tap.

Poured Dettol on the teeth marks to disinfect the bitten flesh.

Once he was confident it was clean, he wrapped a bandage around his hand.

He looked at his face and noticed a few bumps and bruises that hadn't been there an hour or so ago.

McGinty would have a few too.

He had caught him good and proper. Nick Forti's master-class had paid dividends.

If he had had a number, he would have called him. He needed to speak to somebody.

Cain grabbed his keys and about turned out of the apartment. He crossed the A56 onto the Bridge 101 tow path. Behind him hushed loud voices.

'Don't,'

'Fuck off.'

'Don't.'

'Piss off.'

'Give me the knife.'

Instead of heading toward the Manifesto or calling the police, Cain walked under the bridge towards Deansgate Locks.

At the end of the tunnel a boy and girl were having a lover's tiff.

He recognised the girl immediately.

Summer was standing on top of a wooden lock gate

reaching out her hand, precariously balanced on the beam.

Less than a dozen feet from her was a skinny youth. Equally precariously balanced. But with his hand clasping his throat.

Once his eyes had adjusted, Cain recognised Swastika Boy holding a blade to his own throat. His defiant face. Wide eyes focused on Summer. Oblivious to him.

'What's going on?' asked Cain. It was obvious. Swastika Boy was having trouble with himself. Karma had caught up with him. 'What are you doing with him, Summer?'

'He's suicidal,' hissed Summer. 'Call somebody.'

'He ... attacked your mother,' said Cain.

'Don't be daft, he's not black,' said Summer. 'He's taken something. You know him?'

Light rain fell into the canal water. Cain watched the ripples on the water. Live by the knife, die by the knife. Karma did exist. 'He attacked your mother.'

'She was my life,' cried Swastika Boy. 'The only person who ever truly understood me.'

'What do mean?' Summer asked Cain out of the boy's earshot.

'The swastika on his face,' Cain said to Summer. 'The boy who attacked us had the same the tattoo.'

'His girlfriend drowned here earlier this evening.'

Cain glanced to his right. Saw blue and white crime scene tape at the other end the lock.

This was the Rachel Roberts incident he had seen from the rooftop. 'I am sorry to hear that,' Cain said, loud enough for them both to hear. 'Who was she?'

'Rachel. The games we played. The fun we had. Then she had to spoil it all. Why?'

What to do? Walk away and call 999. Pass the problem to the blue light emergency services by carrying out Summer's instructions.

Alternatively, he could try to convince the boy not to cut his own throat.

Nobody would blame him if he turned his back. Not after he'd wrecked his life. His conscience would be clear.

They both turned to look at Cain.

As he twisted his head to the right, the blade punctured the boy's skin and drew blood.

A small stream ran down to his collar.

In the moonlight, Cain saw twins in the young wet silvery faces that would explain April's darkest secret.

If it was true, he could not let the boy kill himself. 'You should put the knife down or throw it in the water,' said Cain.

'Do I know you?' Ryan asked Cain.

Tough question: a little white lie or big black one?

He could play for a confession on the waterfront or make sure the boy was safe.

Pick the right or wrong words and he might save the police, courts and prison service a lot of time and expense, especially if his father's wall of silence let him walk free.

What had Nick asked him?

What did revenge look like?

Letting him kill himself was too easy for everyone.

Cancer took away one scapegoat and let them off the hook for two decades, until the guilt and shame became too much for April.

Imagine having your baby stolen from you by Billy McGinty and his wife?

Thirty-Six.

He should have guessed April's secret when Violet was violently sick at the mention of Eric.

You don't have that reaction over another woman's child. But your own? A stillborn child decomposing inside you. A body too disfigured to let a mother hold and hug.

The pain would have been unbearable, especially if your best friend was lying in the next room with two healthy twins.

What would a gangster and his gangster wife do in such circumstances?

Steal one of them.

They stole everything else in their sad nasty lives so why would pinching a baby be any different.

Bob and April must have been terrified handing over their boy. No wonder he wasn't paying attention when he was driving through Prestwich.

Summer and Ryan might know themselves. Twins have a second sense unique to them. They might make the connections themselves. And if they didn't, they would share the same DNA. At last he had McGinty leverage. You could never deny the science. The more immediate problem was getting Ryan to drop the knife.

'I can understand how you feel, Ryan. I loved a woman once. Loved her so much that it hurt when we weren't together. When we were apart, I wanted to be reunited even if we were only separated by a mile or two or the thin walls in a house. No other woman can come close to the love I felt for her. But just because she decided to take another way out, doesn't mean you have to do the same. People love you. Adore you more than life itself. You owe it to them to stay around. No matter how and you feel or low you get. I was the happiest man in the world when the most beautiful woman in the world said she would marry me. Only a short distance from here. A short while ago. Our engagement was short lived. No longer than it took to watch Manchester United play a game of football. Are you a red or a blue Ryan?'

'Red. Obviously.'

'You?' Cain asked Summer.

'Blue. Everton not City.'

'What happened?' asked Ryan.

Little white lie or a big black one? What did revenge look like? How did it taste? Was it best served cold?

Billy had let him live. Or had decided not to kill him, today.

Cain paused his monologue. Looked briefly at Summer. She got it.

Ryan still held the knife to his jugular. He was oblivious, or was he?

'She went off with another man. A bigger man than me.'

'Who?'

'Summer knows him. Big guy upstairs. Works in the film business in California.'

'Hal Rogers. You like films Ryan?'

'Music ones.'

'My dad made *All Down The Line*.'

'Love that movie. Everyone is soooo fucking stoned.'

'I make movies too. We could remake *All Down The Line* with you and your mates as the drug dealers if you come and have a coffee with me.'

'Nah.'

'You'd be great. You're almost as pretty as me …and that is pretty pretty,' said Summer, 'We could almost be…'

'Has she died?' Ryan asked Cain, as he lifted his head slightly higher and stood slightly taller.

'She's fine. We'll be walking down the aisle soon.'

'I don't believe you.'

'We can go and see her now.'

'You're lying to me.'

'We're not,' Cain and Summer said in unison.

'Rachel said we were brother and sister. I've killed my real mum,' said Ryan.

The knife dropped. Bounced into the water with a slight splash.

The two of them jumped in as the body fell downwards.

Thirty-Seven.

Cain looked out at the sun rising over Manchester. Made a cafetière of coffee for three although there was only one person so drink it.

Summer was still at the hospital. She'd refused point blank to leave or discuss anything.

The plane tickets and a job in the USA were on the table.

He could still leave later this afternoon. Only a fool would stay in Manchester after what had happened to Ryan McGinty.

Billy McGinty would not be as lenient the next time. Knew he could not sucker punch him twice. He had caught him by surprise and would never have that advantage again.

The coffee tasted OK but was not like it used to be. Morning coffee was better shared in conversation with the most beautiful woman in the world.

He called Vince Crane. Asked if he was still interested in buying his share of the restaurant.

'You still flying out later after last night?'

'My only sensible option.'

'I've heard the odd rumour. Give me ten minutes,' said Vince.

He called Cain from downstairs and they were on the road within eight heading the short distance to the Red Manifesto.

They had a couple of hours to thrash out a deal before the cleaning staff and duty managers and team leaders came in at eleven.

Like the apartment, the restaurant was not the same without her.

He could pretend as much as he liked, but it would pure fantasy to recreate perfection.

Vince helped himself to a bottle of Chablis. Cain watched him collect two glasses designed for red rather than white wine.

Vince never entered the wine into the EPOS system. April said pre-dispensing was the only way to stay afloat. But Vince wasn't interested in restaurants. Vince wanted a legit business to clean drug money.

'Cheers. Here's to April. And you. I hope America works out for you both,' said Vince. They clinked glasses and took a sip each

'I'll be straight up with you, Vince, because I want to make a clean break today. My stake is worth £200 grand for the brand name. That gets you a seat at the table and equal voting rights with April's daughter, if she keeps it. The assets belong to her, but you can trade.'

'You want fast cash?' asked Vince. 'A flash sale.'

'Not really. I am talking to you because we're friends. I can keep my investment and manage it from California.'

'From that distance?'

'It's not bloody Mars, mate,' laughed Cain.

'I've done us a contract. Mate of mine works at Simpson & Konest. Done me a favour.' Vince took out two sheets of paper that had been stapled together.

Cain read the numbers. Twelve grand upfront and two and half grand a month for 36 months. He did the sums. He valued his stake at hundred grand, a fifty per cent discount on a sale he didn't need to make. He'd sold his house to buy into the Red Manifesto. It was his bloody pension.

'Sorry, Vince. That's giving it away.'

Vince brought a large envelope. Plonked it hard on the table. 'I'll give you three a month for four years and first buy-back option. Twelve grand cash. My deposit. Count it if you want.'

Cain recognised the bag Vince had pulled it from his jacket pocket. 'I've already counted it. Should be all there unless Rachel Roberts skimmed some off the top.'

'That's my money,' said Vince.

'Where did you get it? Before or after she drowned?'

'You're going to sign the paper one or another. Might as well take the money.'

'Sorry, mate, no can do.' Cain got up. And fell down again. Moved sideways and backwards. Bounced off the wall. Then he was dragged like a cat by the scruff of the neck into the passenger seat of the black Range Rover.

'Every time you speak a word to me, I am going to break a finger. I might even cut them off. So Mr Wordsmith, think very carefully before you open your mouth.'

The noises were distorted in Cain's head. He was disorientated and struggling to make any sense of the violence, probably concussed. Had he lost consciousness, like April? He was aware a mobile phone was ringing. He recognised Billy McGinty's voice.

'Are you travelling with that too tall lanky streak of piss, Vincent?'

'We're going to Monty's container depot in Oldham. Closed today for a funeral. Let yourself in. Shut the gate afterwards. We don't want any prying eyes interfering.'

'Good boy, Vince.'

The line went dead. 'That's not an excuse for you to open your mouth,' said Vince.

In the transport yard, they were surrounded by shipping containers and a small cabin.

Vince parked up and pulled Cain out of the car. Made him kneel with his back to him. 'You can sign the sale document while we wait for Billy. I'll keep the twelve grand. Sign it.'

Cain waited to be hit again. *Everybody had a plan until they got punched in the mouth.* He laughed. Thought what the fuck, it was just pain. He heard a gun slide and cock. He spat blood on the floor. Vince had another plan.

'I have no problem killing people, Cain. First one made me feel a bit queasy, after that bring it on. Might actually be doing you a favour shooting you in the back of the head. Billy's a right old sadist.'

'I'll sign. Twelve grand and you take care of Billy for me. Services in kind. For him and his son killing April.'

'Very tempting offer, Cain, but too late. Billy is a bit of a scumbag, but that's not on him. All down to me. April was having conscience collywobbles. Normally, Rachel reined her in. But when you proposed, she wanted to confess. Pure coincidence Ryan and Liam were on hand. All very rushed. We only had three hours to pull it together to give her a physical telling to keep her mouth zipped. We were all earning good money, but that would implode if everyone knew what she and the McGintys were really like. Chaos is not good for business.'

'What did she want to confess?'

'Selling her boy to make a movie.'

Cain could hear a car engine approaching. Heard it stop while the gates were opened.

He wasn't going to beg. Not in front of Billy McGinty or Vince Crane. They could have his body, but his courage belonged to him.

He turned his head and saw another Range Rover with a trailer park next to Vince's motor.

Billy jumped out. Two Smiles climbed out of the passenger's side and went to the trailer.

Cain heard dogs barking before they were silenced by Two Smiles.

'Why did you bring them for?' asked Vince.

'They need exercising. Not eaten properly for a couple of days,' replied Billy.

'How's Ryan?'

'Hanging in there. Violet's with him. Poor boy was confused.'

'Youngsters. Just say the word, Billy and I'll put one in the back of his head for you,' said Vince.

'Not on the ground. Don't want to leave evidence. Use one of the containers,' said Billy. 'Go and open one up.'

Billy knelt down in front of Cain. Lifted him by the chin. Inspected his face. They were both busted up pretty bad. Cain smiled at the damage he had done. Billy smiled back.

Slapped him gently on the cheek. 'Thank you. From Violet. And from me.'

Cain watched Billy stand up.

Walk over to Vince. 'We want to make it look like a suicide, not an IRA execution. A note confessing to the murders of Rachel Roberts and April Sands would be useful.'

'April's not dead,' said Vince.

'She won't recover, Vince. That shithead is shaking too much to write. You scribble the note and then he can sign it. I'll hold the pistol for you. Might even do it myself.'

Cain stayed on the ground and waited. Billy and Two Smiles talked United while Vince wrote his suicide note.

So, this it. The end. At least he went out on his terms.

It has been a good life, apart from two tragedies, but he wasn't the first to suffer grief, and he would not be the last.

He looked up and hoped Little Miss Red Dress wasn't watching. She didn't need to see her father die.

'Do you want to check it?' asked Vince. He passed the note to Billy. 'I want him to sign over the restaurant to me before he goes on vacation.'

'You're a good writer,' said Billy.

Vince knelt in front of Cain with the paper and a pen and a book to lean on. 'Just your name. And date. You know I heard your proposal speech … that bull about living the rest of your lives in perfect harmony. She was only ever with you out of guilt.'

'Guilt for what?'

'Killing your daughter on the Bury New Road. She drove the car. Selling her own child. One tortured woman with a big mouth.'

'April?'

'Shocking isn't it. Surprised you never guessed. Blinded by love. Sign the paper.'

'Let's get this done,' said Billy. 'Less of the verbals.'

'Did she?' Cain asked Billy.

'Walk towards the container,' said Billy.

'Was it true?'

'I took a vow of silence. Not breaking it now,' said Billy.

Cain stood up. No pleading. Better this than to suffer like Ted Blake or end up half a man like Len Harvey. He walked up a slight ramp into the container.

Vince was in front of him. 'Time to kneel.' His head hit the bridge of Cain's nose.

Cain's knees went and he collapsed to the floor. He heard Two Smiles laugh and dogs bark at the outbreak of violence.

'Fucking hell Vince, it's not a sport.'

'Twat looked down on me.'

'That's because he is taller than you,' said Billy. 'Has he signed the confession?'

'No,' said Cain, blood streamed down his face.

'Come down here, Cain. Vince, you stay in the container.'

Cain made his way out of the container. Saw the dogs. In the flesh, they were far worse than any You Tube video. Twice as big. Three times as ferocious. Four of them.

He stood beside Billy. Reached out for the pen, but his attention was elsewhere. 'Let them go, Liam.'

'KILL.' shouted Two Smiles and he pointed towards Vince in the container. The four dogs charged and hit him like a hurricane. Two Scars shut the doors to muffle the screams. Billy turned on the music in Vince's car and yanked up the volume as the Stones played *Rip This Joint.*

'You want a lift anywhere?'

Goodbye.

The wind blew softly across the humanist burial ground. A slight drizzle fell on the small crowd gathered in open orchard near Ramsbottom on the northside of Manchester.

The breeze and the rain were refreshing after a late Indian summer. The sun fought through the grey clouds.

A rainbow arched over the rolling hills. A multi-coloured tribute to say a final goodbye to the most beautiful woman in the world who also happened to be one of the most tormented.

The mourners followed the wooden hand pulled cart on the short journey to the field. They unloaded the biodegradable wicker casket. Placed the coffin next to a hole in the ground a few yards from a large oak tree.

Sally Port, the celebrant, stepped forward. Welcomed everyone to celebrate the life of April Sands.

Sally said although her body was gone, April would live on in hearts of everyone who was gathered here today. Death was not the end, they were just not there anymore, but you could still talk to them whenever you wanted.

She spoke for ten minutes. Then she invited others to speak and share their experiences.

Summer was the first to step forward, a smile on her face. She spoke softly about how this funeral was not what she would have planned if it was up to her.

Summer would have wanted a religious service so they could talk direct to God as they returned her mother to sit by his side in heaven.

Unfortunately, her mother's wishes were made clear in her will: no fuss, no God, a humanist goodbye.

She said her mother always spoke her mind and had strong convictions about what was right and wrong and that would be one of her lasting legacies that she would pass onto her children when the time was right.

She owned the majority share of the Red Manifesto and would divide her time between running the restaurant and her burgeoning film career.

She was already looking at remaking the film that made her father famous, *All Down The Line*. She was working on a script and looking for funding.

She was mentoring Ryan, a young producer who had crossed his own line.

Her inspiration was and always would be her mother. She looked to the heavens and spoke to God: you took her too soon; maybe you needed her more than we both did.

Bob Ord followed in his daughter's footsteps and was accompanied by a young guitar player and a singer.

Bob said he never stopped loving April despite the fact they could not live together.

He said him and April had come with the idea of the life-changing film when Madchester was at its height and they spent most of their time high as kites, listening to the city's bands, but always returning to Exile at the end of the long evening.

Exile was loose, made purely for the love of music.

Making the movie in France was the best of times, the cast and crew working their metaphorical bollocks off, everyone multi-tasking and helping wherever they could.

April, despite being pregnant with Summer, would cook superb food for the cast and crew.

Every meal was a gastronomic delight served up with a smile and a song.

Their favourite was adapting the lyrics of *All Down The Line* as it applied to the Mancunian upstarts living it large in the south of France in a mansion as far removed from Salford's cobbled streets as you could be: *oh yeah, heard the actors rehearsing, all down the line, oh, heard the cash tills ringing, all down the line, yeah, hear crew chewing, all down the line, oh, hear the boys boozing, all down the line.*

Bob said he would let the music complete his farewell. The duo were the same age as Summer, but that didn't stop them owning *All Down The Line*.

The guests tapped their feet and shuffled on the grass to the strumming six strings, eventually everyone joining in on the chorus asking the listeners to be their babies for a while.

As if it was that easy.

Cain stepped forward.

Said it was a privilege to have April as his best friend, even if it only for such a short while.

He said his words could never do her justice because he was not a good enough writer.

He paused, realised he was in danger of repeating the same words from the night he had proposed to her in the Red Manifesto.

He had all sorts of things planned in his mind, but at the end of the day, he loved her for who she was, good and bad.

Cain said he didn't believe in religion, but he liked to think a dead person's spirit lived on in the people who loved them while they were here.

He pictured Little Miss Red Dress and April, sat by her side, arm around her, protected from the rain by the giant oak.

She'd been punished more than enough for killing Cain's daughter and giving away her own baby, more than any one person ever deserved. No revenge could ever compete.

Billy had given Cain his version of the truth. The most feared gangster in the city had parked up on the roadside in Cheetham Hill. Said it was a one-off conversation that would never be repeated. 'It is what it is,' he said, 'or was.'

April had given away her baby boy to Violet and then regretted it.

They'd been too dumb to do things properly, legally.

Everything else was propaganda.

He let others speak.

Thought of Rita Rock trying to find Vince Crane for the murders of Rachel Roberts and April Sands.

She had accepted Cain's defence that Vince had forced him to mention it was Ryan and Two Smiles.

Rita had shaken her head when he did a new statement, said the world had gone to the dogs.

Cain knew April would have smiled at the irony. Billy would probably have laughed too.

Cain understood his own hypocrisy. He couldn't sell her short. That was too unkind.

One day Vince's relatives might come knocking on Cain's door with their own questions. What happened to our son, brother, uncle, nephew, father?

White Lie, Black Lie? He knows he'll never tell them what really happened. Like Billy, Violet and Bob and their pact.

Truth hurts. Really hurts. But sometimes it was best hidden.

Without Rules

China is fighting back. Knows she must win at all costs or she is mincemeat.

Sexually abused as a young teen, China fears her young daughter is next unless she breaks free from her abusers.

She can only do this if she tears up the rulebook. Becomes more ruthless and deadly than her evil amoral abusers.

When her initial plan ends in a bloodbath, she must quickly devise another way to escape, whatever the price.

Always Adam

London-based financial journalist Spencer Beck is obsessed with billionaire biotech prodigy, Adam Reid, orphaned in his mid-teens when his parents died in a tragic murder-suicide in New York City.

A shadowy informant with MI5 connections promises Beck unfettered access to the mysterious Reid and introduces him to Daniel Flanagan, a retired Big Apple detective who investigated the deaths of Adam's mother and father.

Spencer's initial scepticism, fed by the suspicions of the former police officer, turns to excitement when Reid reveals the truth about himself and his altruistic ambitions to protect society from a deadly virus with a powerful vaccine he's developed.

But when Beck's entire world starts to implode, he discovers Reid harbours a vendetta that, left unchecked, threatens not only his survival but that of an entire species.

Available from Amazon and direct from Boomslang

www.boomslangbooks.org

 **BOOMSLANG**
BOOKS